FORBIDDEN PRINCESS

RETRIBUTION GAMES BOOK 2

ELLA MILES

RETRIBUTION GAMES SERIES

Mistaken Hero
Forbidden Princess
Tempted Hero
Fatal Princess
Tortured Hero
Dangerous Princess

PROLOGUE
BECKETT

THE INFORMATION you need is waiting for you at the Retribution Kings' headquarters.

Corsi's words play in my head over and over.

Odette, I'm coming.

I race out of the Phantom Brotherhood's club as soon as Vincent Corsi's men leave, following Vicent and his daughter. I don't look back to see if Caius and the rest are following me; I just dart out the door. I don't even know where exactly the headquarters is, but I have to get there as fast as possible.

The prospect of finding out what happened to Odette doesn't stop the twinge of guilt from squeezing in my chest as I watch the raven-haired woman with the fierce mouth climb into the car. Her destiny has always been this. Ri couldn't run forever, not from a man like her father.

But it won't sit well with Odette that I sacrificed Ri in order to save her, and I want to be the best man I can for Odette. I'll worry about helping Ri after I get Odette back. She has to be my sole focus now. Ri isn't in any real danger. It's not like her father is going to hurt her; he'll just marry her off to a corrupt monster.

"This way," Gage says, grabbing my arm as we hit the street. He shoves me into the passenger seat of a car and then climbs into the back. Caius is already in the driver's seat while the other three settle into the back; then, we are speeding off.

"How far?" I growl, my hand gripping the handle of the door, ready to jump out the second the car stops.

"Five minutes," Caius responds, driving faster. He wants to find out what happened to his sister as much as I do.

My knee bounces up and down rapidly. I've spent a week without Odette.

A week spending every moment looking for her.

A week worrying about the danger she was in.

A week without sleep.

A week not knowing if she was alive.

A week wondering if she even loves me.

I'm about to find out the truth.

My agreement with Vincent is that he will provide me the information and resources to get her back. She might very well be at the headquarters, and if not, then at least I'll finally have the information I need to get her back.

Then, I can face my future. Then, I can find out if my love is enough. *Does she truly want me? Or did she just marry me out of duty to her family, to the Retribution Kings?*

Caius stops the car on the side of the road. I throw the door open and run into the skyscraper. I make it to the elevator banks before anyone else and hit the button repeatedly while the rest catch up before the doors finally open.

We pile in, and Lennox hits the button for the fifteenth floor.

I close my eyes, thinking of Odette's smile on our wedding day. It seemed so genuine, so true. *But was it?*

My hands shake, my brow drips in sweat, and my heart —oh, my fucking heart doesn't know whether it's finally about to heal or break into a million pieces.

The doors open, and I rush out, not having a clue where I'm going, but it doesn't stop me. We are on an office floor. I pass cubicles until I find what looks like an important office.

The door is locked.

There's no time.

I break the door down before Caius has time to get a key out. Their heavy breaths behind me tell me I'm right — this is the office I should be breaking down doors to enter.

Odette isn't in the room.

There is a manila envelope on the desk. I grab it and shove my hand inside to pull out the contents—a letter and a picture. The picture is lying on top of the letter, and it drops me to my knees.

I let out a guttural scream, the kind that if this were a movie, I'd release a great shadow over the world, create a mystical monster out of my grief, or at the very least shatter every piece of glass in this building.

None of that happens, but it feels the same leaving my body.

The scream goes on and on until I'm shaking and tears wreck my body. But I don't let go of the picture or the letter. I need to read the letter, but I can't, not yet.

My chest heaves, rising and falling rapidly as I grip the

picture tighter and stare at my beautiful wife lying on a concrete floor with her brains blown out.

I squeeze my eyes shut, trying to remember Odette before this picture, but this is the image that will haunt me. And I deserve to be haunted.

I saved the wrong girl. I wasted time believing that Ri was the key to finding Odette, when I should have found Odette on my own. I should have spent every moment on her. I deserve to be punished.

The room slowly comes back into my view.

I don't know how long I've been kneeling in pain. Tears continue to speed down my face like hot oil, and my agony tears through my lungs with each excruciating scream.

Lennox is the only one still standing. He rubs his face, not looking at anyone, afraid he'll completely break if he does. Gage and Hayes are gripping onto each other as they quietly sob.

But Caius—he sits stone-faced, his back leaning against the wall of windows. If he cried or showed any emotion, it has long left his face.

"Who was it?" Caius asks, his voice cool as ice.

I stare at the photo. There is no obvious evidence of where she died or who shot her. She's still in her wedding dress, which somehow makes it worse. My blood boils thinking about the life we could have had together—if only. So many if onlys.

"My guess is Corsi," Lennox says, wiping his tears on the back of his shirt sleeve.

The room silently nods its agreement, but I shift my focus to the letter and read Corsi's assessment.

.   .   .

We found her body in the basement of the Phantom Brother-hood. She died the night of your wedding. They took no chances. Ares knew he couldn't get my daughter to marry him and that I would never honor an alliance between his crew and my empire. But he knew that you were powerful enough to pique my interest. He thought that with your wife dead, you would be happy to marry my daughter and form an alliance that would benefit him. As you know, I ensured that Ares met his fate. And you have my blessing to seek retribution against the entire Phantom Brotherhood.

You have my sympathy on the loss of your wife and my gratitude for the safe return of my daughter. It's been a pleasure working with you.

—*Vincent Corsi*

I crumple up the piece of paper and toss it at the door with a growl.

All eyes fall on me.

"Corsi blames Ares."

"No way. That bastard didn't have the balls or the fore-sight to take her and kill her," Hayes says.

Everyone mumbles their agreement.

"It has to be Corsi," I say.

I stand up, pacing the room as I think through what happens next.

"Of course it was Corsi," a deep voice says from the doorway.

Slowly, my eyes drift to him, scared to death to face this man. He's wearing slacks and a sharp buttoned-down shirt. A cane at his side helps him stand, a cane he wasn't using at the wedding. His gray hair seems to have whitened, and the lines around his eyes seemed to have deepened overnight. He's frailer than he was a week ago. That's what your impending death will do to you. And I suspect the news of his daughter's death with be what finishes him.

I open my mouth, but I can't speak. I can't tell him. I've barely accepted the truth myself, and only because I have the damn picture.

"I know my daughter's dead. I was working in the conference room. I heard your screams—people only make that sound when they lose the other half of their soul," Michael Monroe, Odette's father says.

"Sir, I'm so sorry. I failed at protecting her. I'm not worthy—"

"Shush," he silences me as he steps into the room with a strength I don't understand. He picks up the crumpled paper, and then walks over to take the picture I still grip in my hand. He slowly loosens my grip to remove the picture. I should stop him from looking; it will break him.

But he doesn't shed a tear. If others observed a father not crying at the loss of his daughter, they might call him cold, heartless, a monster. But Michael Monroe is none of those things. He's just strong. He has to be in order to be the leader of the Retribution Kings.

After studying the picture and letter, he looks to me. "What will you do for my daughter now?"

"I will get retribution. I will go to the ends of the earth to ensure everyone who had a hand in her death pays for their crime. I will ensure she rests in peace."

"Good, you're ready."

"What?"

He puts his hands on both of my shoulders and stares

deep into my eyes. "Do you know why they call us Retribution Kings?"

I shake my head. "Because we believe revenge is more powerful than blood. We vow to set wrongs right. We aren't the good guys. Instead, we get revenge like kings. We derive our power from taking vengeance against those who cross us. And we always get justice. Anyone who crosses us always pays—usually, with their life. You seeking retribution for Odette, your incredible loss, makes you the perfect man to lead us."

"You still want me to...to take your place as leader?"

"Yes, I have no doubt. Your initiation will start soon, but your final task will be to get retribution for Odette. Do that and my kingdom is yours."

"I don't want—"

He shakes his head. "Being the king of the Retribution Kings is an honor and a burden. You're going to need their help, and they're going to need you. And you're going to need a purpose when this is all over."

I look at Caius, who still hasn't broken, just like his father. He should be the leader. But I need to do this. I need to be the one to bring Vincent, his men, Ri, and every other person involved in Odette's death to justice.

Me.

I can't leave it to Caius. I have to be the one. So if it means I get the power when it's over, then so be it. I'll do whatever it takes, even if I have to betray them all to honor Odette in her death.

"How do you plan on getting retribution? How do we find out who did this? How do we make them pay?" Caius asks me.

They all have more experience at getting revenge in

this town, but as I stare into all of their hardened eyes, I know that we can do this together.

"I have an idea—a game."

Their lips twist up in wicked curls.

"A way to ruin Corsi, his family, any men involved, and Ri."

I wait for them to defend her, to say she had nothing to do with this. But none of them come to her defense.

I tell them my idea, and together we brainstorm the best way to execute it.

A contest to take them all down.

The best way to get to Corsi is through Ri. The best way to make the others weak is Ri. Whether Ri is involved or not—she will pay a price.

I'll convince him to start a game. A game that will help him control his rivals and prevent an all-out war that Monroe said has been brewing. A game I can win.

Win his daughter.

His empire.

Then destroy them all.

We have a plan. Now it's time to execute. I pick up my phone and call Corsi, hoping he still thinks I'm on his side and that I want to offer my thanks instead of carve his heart out.

———

I tip back the burning scotch. The alcohol is the only thing keeping me going at this point. It's the only thing keeping me from crumbling to the ground and dissolving in a puddle of my own tears.

A waiter quickly refills my glass. I'm sure Corsi told the staff to keep the alcohol flowing—a sure-fire way to get these men to fall into his hands and the plan I gave him. He invited us all here—every gangster, elite, monster in the city. We are all here. Now it's time to see if he enacts my plan as his own.

This time the scotch barely burns my throat as I take another gulp. It numbs my feelings remarkably well, but it doesn't erase the image in my head. I can only see the image of Odette lying on the floor with a bullet in her head.

I don't even have her body—nothing to bury.

I will find her.

I will get retribution.

I will destroy them all.

I lean back in my chair as I adjust my tie. The tux is scratchy and suffocating, but it's a necessary facade to play the role. Corsi thinks I want his daughter, that I'll prove myself worthy during this game. He doesn't know I'm playing him like a pawn. I'm using them both to find out what happened to Odette and bring her body home to rest. And if he or his daughter are in any way responsible, as I suspect, I'll burn everything he loves to the ground.

Gage eyes me as I finish another drink. His scowl says I've had enough, but he doesn't speak his judgment. He doesn't realize there is no way for me to get drunk, not when my heart aches like it does. My heart ensures that I stay sober.

My eyes drift to the others at the table. Gage's tux fits him perfectly. Hayes is wearing a navy blue suit, looking cool and sharp in it. Lennox is wearing a gray suit, but he's already removed the jacket. His sleeves are rolled up like he doesn't give a shit that this is supposed to be a black-tie affair.

And Caius sits perfectly still in his tux. He still hasn't

shown any emotion, not one damn tear. He's barely spoken as well. Everyone mourns in different ways, but a tidal wave is waiting to crush him the moment he finally lets himself feel.

The doors at the back of the ballroom suddenly open, and Corsi and Rialta walk in surrounded by their guards. Corsi wears a tux that exudes his power and wealth, signaling that he is the king. Rialta shines as a dark princess in her slinky black lace dress that exposes the skin around her sides and swirls around her hips, leaving a train of sparkly lace at the back. Her tiara sits firmly on her head, and she walks without fear by her father's side.

My eyes lock on her as she walks, studying her closely, trying to understand if she is the broken daughter of a monster afraid for her life and future, or if she's a proud, dangerous princess who willingly does her father's bidding.

She's fooled me before; I won't let her fool me again. I try to look through to her heart to see if it's as black as her father's, but I can't tell.

They walk up onto the stage at the end of the room. And then Vincent Corsi starts speaking.

"Thank you all for gathering. As you know, we have several important things to discuss. First, I'd like you to celebrate the safe return of my daughter, Rialta Corsi."

The crowd starts applauding, but I don't. No one at my table does. Maybe we should to avoid any blowback, but there will be no cheering or happiness until I have the man who killed Odette's blood on my hand.

"Now, for the less than happy news. As you all know, Rialta was set to be married to Nicolo Ricci on her twenty-first birthday."

The room drops silent, and Rialta's eyes widen in

terror. The room is so quiet that I swear I can hear her heartbeat even from here. She's petrified.

Good.

"But it is with a heavy heart that I have to report that Nicolo has been murdered."

Corsi probably murdered him just so the bastard could arrange this game. When I called him, I could hear his giddiness at the thought of being able to control so many men at once.

"My daughter's safety has been at risk over this last week, but the Retribution Kings ensured her safe return. And they helped me create a plan for how to keep her safe forever."

Corsi nods his head toward me to offer his thanks. I merely look at him with a bored expression, like saving his daughter meant nothing to me.

"My daughter is in need of a husband, one who will keep her safe."

Here we go.

"With such a prize as my daughter at stake, there are bound to be fights breaking out. So to ensure the best man for the job wins, I've devised a game. It will keep my daughter safe and prevent fighting amongst ourselves outside of the game. The winner gets to marry my daughter."

I watch in twisted enjoyment as Rialta squirms on the stage. My sinister heart grins as she tries to get her panicked breathing under control.

Maybe she isn't her father's stooge? Maybe she truly is innocent?

Doesn't matter, not anymore. Odette's gone.

"I'm sure you are wondering what the rules are, but that will have to wait. For now, know this—any man here can enter, only one will win. If you enter and lose...well, I don't recommend losing." He smirks.

The crowd chuckles in response to his joke. No one at my table laughs.

"Enter however many men from your gang that you dare, but you must follow my rules. If you don't, there will be consequences." He snaps his fingers, and an image appears on a screen behind us of Ares dead from a gunshot.

The image doesn't bring me any comfort because I don't believe that Ares killed Odette. The image fades.

"There are cards on your table. If you would like to enter the game, sign your name in blood, and then bring your card to the stage. Place it in the bowl in my beautiful daughter's hands."

A bowl is placed in Rialta's trembling hands.

Oh, my beautiful Princess, how I'm going to enjoy breaking you.

I turn to my table as men at surrounding tables start rushing to put their names in the bowl in Rialta's hands. Stupid fools think they have a shot at winning this game. All that awaits them is shame, pain, and probably death.

I grab one of the cards in the middle of the table. I prick my thumb with my pocketknife and sign my name on the card.

A movement catches my attention out of the corner of my eye.

"What are you doing?" I demand.

"Entering," Caius says coldly.

"You don't get to enter. As your leader, I forbid it."

"You can't stop me."

He stands up. I do as well, getting in his face.

"If you want to remain in the Retribution Kings, you will do as I say. Sit down."

"No, Odette was my sister. I deserve retribution as much as you do. If we both enter, we have twice the spies in this game, twice the chances of winning. I have to do this for Odette."

I breathe loudly.

I don't like it, but I can see his grief hiding in the shadows. He'll let it explode out of him if I don't let him enter. He needs this as much as I do.

I step out of his way. I'll let him enter, but it doesn't mean I'll let him win. Rialta is *mine*. Mine to win. Mine to torture. Mine to destroy.

Caius walks up on the stage, and I turn to the rest of the guys. "Don't even think about entering."

Then I follow him up on the stage.

Rialta doesn't notice me at first. She's too upset about Caius entering, recognizing that this a bloodshed game as much as it is a game for her heart.

But then she spots me.

Her breath catches. Her heart pumps louder. Her lustful gaze quickly turns to rage as her jaw tightens.

I stop right in front of her.

Her eyes widen in shock, and a deep frown mars her pretty lips.

"Did you find Odette?"

I don't answer her. Instead, I hold my hand out over the bowl.

She blinks, not registering what I'm doing until I release my grip and my card drops into the bowl.

Her eyes look deep into mine, not understanding why in the hell I would enter. It takes her a moment, her eyes racing back and forth, trying to read my face.

Odette's dead, her eyes shoot into me as she realizes.

I give the tiniest of nods. I'm not even sure she notices, but her reaction is real, authentic. She didn't know that Odette was dead. Whatever role she played, she didn't know that Odette was killed as a result.

What game are you playing, Princess?

I can see her mind whirling with thoughts, trying to figure out my endgame, but quickly her gaze shifts.

Hope—I see hope in her eyes.

She wants me to win. Wants me to play hero. Wants me to save her.

If she thought I was cold before, she has no idea who I am now. Odette made me a better man. Without her, there is nothing left of me but a cruel, cold heart. I'm a man set on revenge, revenge Rialta can help me with. If she's waiting on me to play hero, she's going to be waiting a long time.

I lean in and whisper, "I call these the Retribution Games. I'm about to kill everyone that had anything to do with her death. Sorry if a little blood splatters on your pretty tiara, Princess."

She shivers as my words cover her.

Be afraid, Princess, be very afraid. You think I'm better than the rest of these pricks, but you're wrong. There is nothing left but the devil's soul inside me, and I plan on unleashing it upon the world.

1

RI

ENTERING the game won't heal Beckett. It won't heal Caius. It won't heal any of them. They think they can get revenge on me, my father, or anyone else who might have been involved in Odette's death. Maybe they should, but it won't stop their pain, their grief.

How do I know?

I feel like somehow I've already lived through something like it, like I already know their pain. It probably has to do with the fact that I'm standing on stage in a dress I didn't pick out, and holding a bowl full of names of men, one of who gets to marry me. My choices, my life, have been completely taken away from me.

I understand a little bit of grief. I didn't lose my other half; I just lost myself.

More men put their names into the bowl, and every time I pray that none of the other Retribution Kings enter. Sure, I'd love to up my odds of ending up with one of them. Any of them—Hayes, Gage, and even Lennox— would be better than a complete stranger, but I don't want them to risk their lives for me.

"Any other participants?" my father steps forward and says.

I hold my breath, waiting to see if anyone else will enter. I've barely paid attention to who has entered, except to ensure that none of my guys did.

My guys—ha. They aren't mine.

"Good, then I must ask anyone who didn't enter to leave."

I exhale my worry. At least Hayes, Gage, and Lennox are safe.

The room fills with the sound of chairs scraping and good wishes murmured as the room clears out. Soon, only the guys who have decided they want to compete for me are left.

My father walks to me and takes the bowl from my hands. He quickly counts the number of cards and then sets the bowl down on the floor.

"Thirty-three," my father says with no reaction to the number.

Thirty-three, my heart moans. *How many of them are going to survive this game?*

The world will be better off with most of these monsters gone.

I just need two to survive.

My father walks to me and grabs my elbow, leading us toward the center of the stage. The lights are still blinding me to the crowd. I can't see any of them, but I know all of their eyes are on me.

I want to shiver, but I won't allow them to see my fear. I'll figure a way out of this. I hold my head high, my eyes piercing the darkness, trying to strike each of their hearts with daggers.

"The deal is simple. It's the same one I offered Nicolo. You prove worthy of my daughter, and you get the honor of marrying her. You get my blessing. And if you produce a male heir, you get my kingdom the day the child is born."

There is a collective gasp; even I catch my breath. This means whomever I marry is going to fuck me over and over relentlessly until we produce a male child. And if we have daughters, I can't think what someone might do to them.

Fuck, I have to find a way out.

It's one thing to hurt me; it's another to hurt an innocent child.

"What about if we knock her up with a boy before we marry her?" someone dares to heckle from the crowd.

My father gives a stern look. He pulls out a gun and fires into the crowd.

The crowd goes silent. I have no idea if he just shot someone or just shot fear into them.

I don't dare move. He won't shoot me; he needs me. But there is no way he could tell who he was shooting, so he clearly doesn't care.

Please, let Beckett and Caius be alive.

"The terms are the same as I had with Nicolo. Sex is forbidden until I give you permission. She is off-limits in that way, and I'll be checking."

The screen behind us turns back on like this is a presentation he planned with visuals.

The room is beyond silent as a man speaks from the speakers behind me.

"Spread your legs and scoot down to the edge of the bed for me, dear."

Don't look, a voice from deep inside whispers.

But my mind twists with too many images of what my father could be playing.

"That's a good girl."

Every hair on my arms rises. I've heard that voice before.

My hands clench as my breathing shallows.

Don't look.

I have to look.

Slowly, I turn around to face the screen. And it's as evil as my worst nightmares.

I'm lying on a bed, the same bed I stayed in last night. My legs are spread on the edge of the bed, and there's a man dressed as a doctor between them. My father and two other men observe from the door.

"Hymen looks to still be intact," the doctor says, removing a gloved finger from my body.

I stare at myself. *How old was I?*

Eighteen? Nineteen? Younger? I can't tell.

But there is no fear in my eyes. No tears as I lie on that bed, which I can't say is true now.

I feel the tears welling. The violation pulses through my body even now.

The screen pauses.

"Rialta is to remain a virgin until I say otherwise. She will remain that way to ensure her offspring are worthy of my kingdom. Don't fuck her without my permission. I'll know."

I blink, and a tear escapes, rolling quickly down my cheek. I should brush it away before turning back around. I don't want these guys to see my shock, but I leave the tear on my cheek.

My father knows I'm not a virgin; he's seen the proof himself. Hopefully, that sex video will keep me from having to do another one of those virginity tests that apparently filled my youth.

I need a drink to get through the rest of this. Before my father or anyone else can stop me, I dart down the stairs. Only once the darkness consumes me do I wipe the tears from my face. On the main floor my sight is better than onstage. I walk to the first table, where there are several vacant seats and leftover drinks.

I pick up the first and down it, barely registering the scotch's burn as it goes down. I pick up a second and down it, too, as my father continues talking.

"This game is to find out one thing—who is worthy of my daughter. Who is strong enough to lead my family. Each week we will meet. I'll draw a name. That name will take part in creating the game, the rules. But ultimately, I'll be the one deciding how the game is played." He drones on talking of rules, expectations, logistics, and on and on.

The alcohol has barely hit my stomach when it hits me.

I grab one of the pieces of paper, jot my name down, prick my finger, and smear my own blood on the card. If they have a chance to win me, to win my father's kingdom, then I want the same chance.

I storm back onstage, determined to not let my father stop me. He wouldn't dare let on that he doesn't have complete control over me, not in front of them.

He doesn't react. Even his eyebrows don't so much as raise as I walk over to the bowl and drop my card into it. I look him dead in the eyes.

"I get to compete too. And if I win, I get to choose who my husband is."

He only gives me the slightest of nods. I know I have

no chance of winning. He'll rig it so I don't, but I have to try. It's all I've got.

Then I walk back off the stage, my head spinning as memories come flooding back.

2

RI

"Rialta, time to go," Dario, one of the security guards, says to me suddenly.

I don't fight Dario as he leads me away from the now empty ballroom. The lights are on, so I can see the vacant seats and empty alcohol glasses.

I pause when goosebumps crawl up my spine as I look at one particular table. It's the only table with five empty chairs—the table that Beckett and his crew sat at.

"This way," Dario says, grabbing my elbow and guiding me out of the ballroom. He leads me out to the back of the waiting limo.

I slide in and jump when my father speaks, "That was foolish."

"No, it wasn't," I snap back.

"Now you will have to compete the same as them. These games will be deadly. There is no guarantee, even with your skillset, that you'll survive them."

I frown. *My skillset? What is he talking about?*

I try to keep a blank face. I don't want him to know

that I don't remember much, even as the memories seem to be returning.

"Maybe you should change the game, make it less dangerous."

My father huffs.

It was worth a shot to keep Caius and Beckett safe.

"Maybe I'll die, and you'll have no one to whore out and get heirs to your throne," I spit out with glee.

He stares at his phone as he types. "Just stay alive."

"Oh, how sweet. You care about me, huh, Father?"

He cocks his head as if I revealed something, but he doesn't say what.

The car stops back at his condo building. Dario opens the door for me, while the driver opens the door for my father. We head into the elevator alone. Apparently, the guards aren't allowed to ride in the same elevator as us.

The doors open into his condo. I want nothing more than to run upstairs and get out of this dress and heels. But that room...I can't go back to the room where I was violated.

My father starts to walk away, loosening his tie, clearly done with this conversation.

"Did you kill Odette?"

He pauses and turns, looking at me with a savage grin. "Are you proposing a deal?"

"What do you mean?"

His eyes turn to slits as he muses at me. "I knew it."

I stand taller, trying to not let him intimidate me. He won't kill me, but he could hurt me.

"Usually, our deals are where I offer up information in exchange for you owing me a debt."

I shouldn't make a deal with the devil. I know that. But

I need to know. Caius needs to know. Beckett needs to know.

"Tell me the truth."

"I didn't kill Odette. I found her. I conveyed that information to the Retribution Kings." He turns to leave. "I'll let you know when I plan on collecting my debt."

"I won't do it. I won't do any of it. You can't force me to marry another man."

If Odette is really dead, if he really didn't kill her, then there is nothing for me here.

I'll escape.

I'll run again.

The only reason I came back was to help Beckett find Odette. She's gone.

"Do I have to remind you what's at stake? Of who I have? Who I'll hurt if you don't?"

My eyes widen as terror spreads through my body. *Who is he talking about?* The condescending look on his face tells me he knows I don't remember. Pieces are starting to come back, but not this.

He has someone I love, or is using my lack of memory against me. Either way, I can't risk it. I need to be sure I'm not condemning someone I love to death if I leave.

A much younger face flashes in my head. A headache hammers through me like lightning and thunder, striking once and leaving a pounding in its wake. I'm running from him with a gash in my side, covered in blood. It could be one of my father's security guards, but I don't think it is.

"You weren't the one I was running from," I say, barely louder than a whisper.

"Why would you run from me? I keep you safe. At least until the wedding day. Then you aren't my problem anymore."

I rub my head, the pounding intensifying. I need to rest, to give my brain time to process all the returning images.

"You shouldn't do so many drugs, Rialta. It can really fuck up your memories."

I glare at him.

"I remember everything," I say, having no clue if it's true or not.'

"Then you remember our past deals?"

I raise my chin. "Yes."

But do I remember everything? Will I?

He starts to walk away.

"Am I a prisoner here, Father? Or am I allowed to leave this castle in the sky?"

He stops. "Just stay alive until the game is over. And lay off the drugs. I'd hate if you didn't remember our history."

I frown, having no clue how he knows my memories are still fuzzy.

"You started calling me Vincent instead of Father when you were five." He turns and walks away.

My two guards step out of the shadows, prepared to follow me. I reluctantly walk upstairs to my room, pausing at the door, my heart racing. My legs tremble as I stare at the bed where I was violated by that doctor. *What other atrocities have I forgotten?*

"Is there a problem?" Dario asks.

I ignore him and step into the room. I slam my door in his face, before crumpling to the floor.

If Vincent truly didn't kill Odette, then who did? Ares? Someone else?

Memories of my childhood, waitressing, attending college classes all rush through me. I try to find the person I love in my memories. There are friends, co-workers, a crush—none that I feel love toward. So instead, I shift my focus to the man who was chasing me. Deep grey eyes, sharp jawline, flared nostrils, a look of hunger on his face. I don't know his name, his hair color, the build of his body. The clearest feature I see is his stare—hungry, vicious, and wanting.

Who are you?

3

RI

THE GREY-COLORED eyes have been haunting me day and night. *Who are you?* I keep trying to convince my memories to reveal more. This guy is important. He was chasing me. I ran through Beckett and Odette's wedding. I hid in the hotel. I was covered in blood. He could have had something to do with Odette's death.

But I can't remember more than the fear as I ran. I couldn't stop. I swore I'd never stop. That's how dangerous this man is to me.

Why would he target both me and Odette? Two princesses, heirs to turf and power and men. But we are only valuable alive. *Why kill us? And is he coming back to kill me too?*

Maybe because he's dead?

I don't have a laptop, a phone, or anything to search for him on. But maybe I don't need an internet connection to find a picture of him. My best guess is that it was Nicolo, my dead fiancé.

The room is void of any pictures on the walls, but maybe I left something in one of the drawers. I pull open my nightstand drawer and rummage through notebooks, gum wrappers, a vibrator. Then I find what I'm looking for —a single polaroid.

I pull out the picture and examine it closely. This has to be Nicolo.

I study the picture, trying to feel anything, any memories, good or bad, but I get nothing. The picture isn't posed, taken without his consent or knowledge as he walks down the street. He's turning his head, looking right at the camera just in time for this picture to be taken.

He has short dark hair, an angry scowl, and he's wearing a dark suit. The camera's old technology reddened his eyes in the picture, so I have no idea if they are the grey eyes that have been haunting me or not.

Dammit.

I let the photo drop.

There are no other clues for me to find in this bedroom. As the first round of the competition grows closer, I need information and allies if I want to survive and win.

I walk in my pajama pants to my bedroom door and press an ear to the door. I hear Vincent's cronies talking outside. Two guards guard my door day and night. I'm not sure if they are to keep me in or to keep others out.

But I have to try something. I have to know if Beckett and the others are still on my side, or if I'm truly alone in this game.

I open the door, and both men's eyes immediately drop to my breasts. The tank I'm wearing is thin, and I'm sure my nipples are visible beneath the fabric.

"I'm sure Vincent would be thrilled to know that his cronies are checking out his daughter."

I push my breasts out further, and their eyes snap up. "What can we do for you, Rialta?"

"I'd like to see my friend Lucy. If I remember correctly, she works this afternoon at the Red June Cafe."

"Of course. We'll be ready to go when you are."

I shut the door in complete shock. I'm truly not a prisoner here. They are here to keep me safe and alive.

I remember my life before. I was a college student, undeclared major, working at a local restaurant. I lived in a small apartment with Lucy. Dario and Leone watched from afar but were always watching.

Where were they that night that I was attacked? Why didn't they stop him? Would Odette still be alive if they did?

I shower and get dressed as I ponder all those thoughts. I could ask them, but I'm not sure they'd answer. And I don't want them to know what I'm up to. They work for Vincent, not me.

But it's not their loyalty I care about. *Beckett, Caius, Gage, Hayes, and Lennox—are we still on the same side?*

———

They drive me to the cafe without questioning me but stop me before I can get out.

"Here, wear this," Leone says, holding something shiny out to me.

I study it cautiously, like it's going to bite me. It's a sparkly bracelet with hundreds of diamonds.

"No thanks, it doesn't really go with my attire." I'm dressed casually in skinny jeans, a maroon v-neck, and shoes I can run in. I blow-dried my hair in long waves and put on only minimal makeup.

"If you want to get out of this car, you'll put it on," he growls.

I relent, taking the bracelet from his calloused hand. I don't have to ask why he wants me to wear it. It's clear that it has a tracker in it.

I fasten it around my wrist loosely, staring at the ugly piece of jewelry, unsure of how it is going to fit into my plan.

"We'll be watching the perimeter to keep you safe."

"To keep me safe or to keep me from running?" I mumble under my breath as I climb out of the car.

"Safe—you can't run from us," Leone winks.

I roll my eyes before heading inside, not sure what I'm going to find, but hoping that Lucy isn't upset that I haven't called her or worked any of my shifts.

"Well, look who came back from the dead," Lucy says as soon as I enter the small cafe.

Her blonde curls hang down just to her shoulders, her green eyes pierce me with a glare, and her hands are on her hips, just above where her apron sits.

I bite my lip. "I'm sorry I didn't text or call, my life—"

She wraps me in a hug. "Shhh, you don't have to explain."

I melt into her hug, my shoulders slumping, and I exhale a deep breath. She's my friend and I'm safe here, I realize as more memories flood back in my brain. I breathe in her bright, flowery scent.

"Frank, I'm taking my break," Lucy says as she puts her hands on my shoulders, studying me closely like she knows I won't tell her the entire truth of what I've been through. Not yet.

She leads me over to a secluded small table in the back corner. She pushes me into a seat.

"I'll be right back." And then she heads behind the cafe counter.

I purse my lips and blow out several slow breaths as I stare at the bracelet and out through the window. I don't see my shadows, but they're there. I turn my attention back to Lucy, who mumbles something to the guy she's working with.

Frank—she said, but I don't remember him. He must be new.

She comes back carrying two lattes and a piece of chocolate cake.

I raise my eyebrows as she sinks into the chair opposite of me.

She stabs a fork into the enormous piece of cake. "I thought we'd need this after you tell me what happened to your ass this last week."

I take the second fork and take a bite. The fudge frosting combined with the moist chocolate cake is delicious. It melts in my mouth. I'm going to get a stomachache from this amount of sweets, but I don't care.

Lucy lifts her latte to her mouth. "Your father?"

I nod, trying to remember how much I've told her in the past. *How much does she know about this part of my life?*

I look around at the quaint cafe as happy memories flood me, including us blaring music after we close the cafe for the night. We'd dance while we cleaned and closed up. We'd drink a bottle of wine together and eat this very same chocolate cake as we talked about the college guys we wanted to date. The ones she would go after, but I never would because I knew what I was risking —their lives.

"I'm guessing I'm fired after not showing up all week."

"Nah, Ezra loves you. He doesn't care that I've had to work the cafe on my own because you weren't here."

"Thank you"

Lucy shrugs. "It's what best friends are for."

I smile at that.

"Do you remember who came into the cafe that day? The man who chased me?"

She frowns. "No, I'm sorry. One minute you were here, the next you were gone."

I mindlessly take another bite of cake.

"I called you in sick to your summer classes, but I doubt you'll be able to catch up. I told you not to take summer classes anyway."

I was taking an art class and a business class. I'm starting my junior year in the fall and still haven't decided my major, probably because I never thought I'd make it this far. I thought I'd be dead or taken or married off to some cruel man.

"But what you really owe me for is walking Loki."

I laugh just imagining tiny Lucy trying to wrangle Loki, my Great Dane. Well, actually, he's her Great Dane. Lucy claims to hate dogs, but I know she feels safer with him there, even if he isn't the best guard dog.

"Thank you, for everything."

Lucy rolls her eyes. "Don't get all soft on me now."

I sip my latte. It's like I have two different lives—this one as a normal college student and the other one full of dangerous men. As much as I want to sit here all day and catch up with Lucy, I can't.

"Can I borrow your phone?" I ask.

She leans forward, narrowing her eyes at me.

"What?" I puzzle at her reaction.

"You lost your memories again, didn't you?"

We stare back and forth at each other, while I try to decide if I should just be completely honest with her.

"Yes, how do you know?"

"Because you have half a dozen burner phones stashed here and another dozen at our apartment."

"Oh." I grab my head. "I guess my memories are still fuzzier than I thought."

"Tell me everything."

So I do. I tell her about the blood, about Beckett and the guys, about Ares, Paxton. I tell her about Odette, about my father, about the damn game. It all spills out of me— every detail.

"Jesus, girl, you know how to attract drama."

I smile tightly.

She reaches across the table and puts her hand on my wrist as I grip my coffee cup.

"What do you need me to do?"

"I can't get you involved in this."

She chuckles. "I'm already involved. This isn't the first time you've been kidnapped or had your life threatened, hence the burner phones. I've helped you before; I'll help you again."

"But I don't want to put you in danger."

She shakes her head. "That's why you made me take those self-defense classes and carry mace wherever I go. Besides, no one cares about me, even as bait to get to you. They've tried taking me before. It didn't work out. They only want you."

I frown, not liking any of it.

"Let me help you for selfish reasons. If you die or get married off, then there is no way I can afford rent. Plus, I don't think Loki and I will both survive if you're gone."

I smile at that. Then I grab her hand with mine, and I roll my bracelet from my hand to hers.

She doesn't question me. She really is used to this. I see the darkness we have experienced together in her eyes. I've been taken far longer than a week. I was gone a month once without a trace. She did everything she could to find me then.

"I'm going to the bathroom. I won't let you help me," I say, in case my bodyguards have audio. I squeeze her hand, realizing she's the one Vincent threatened if I don't do as he says. Her life is at risk. She's the only person in my life I care about.

Lucy mouths, *be careful.*

I nod.

Then I walk toward the back of the kitchen, where I stashed my burner phones. I pocket one and exit through the back door. I don't spot either bodyguard as I run through the alleyways behind the buildings.

Now, time to figure out how to put myself in danger. If only I could get kidnapped on demand.

RI

I START WALKING as I try to figure out a plan. I'm making this all up as I go along, but I know I need allies. Lucy is one; now, to find out if the Retribution Kings are still others I can count on. I don't know how to get in contact with them, though. I could hang around Caius's place and wait for them to show up, but I don't want to get them in trouble. Vincent's men will be monitoring them all closely.

No, I need a plausible reason to run into them, something I could tell Vincent. Something he'd believe.

I need to get kidnapped.

I need to be in danger.

I need them to save me.

Ares is dead, although I could try heading back to the Phantom Brotherhood's club. However, I doubt they would let me inside after what Vincent did to Ares.

I could try Paxton and Mayhem, but...my back stiffens just thinking about it. I won't let that man touch me ever again.

I think of the grey-eyed man—the man haunting me. Now would be a great time for him to make an appearance. But as I keep wandering, no one attacks me. No van pulls up beside me to throw me inside. No danger approaches.

I stop suddenly, knowing I need a plan. Even though I passed the tracking device off to Lucy, it won't take long for Dario and Leone to realize what I did. Vincent has unlimited resources. I don't have much time before he finds me.

"Sorry," a guy says as his backpack bumps into my shoulder.

I smile casually at him, and then I look around at where I've stopped. College students are weaving their way through large grassy areas as old buildings tower around them.

When I let myself wander, I found my way back here, to the life I've always wanted. A normal life where I could be a normal college student where my only fears were whether I was going to fail my calculus test, not who was going to kidnap me, or which asshole I was going to be forced into marrying.

Being here doesn't help me get kidnapped, though. It doesn't put my life in danger.

"Party at Cameron's cabin tonight," a guy shoves a flyer into my hands.

I start to crumple it up and throw it away when I decide to study it closer. Maybe I don't need to get kidnapped by a monster; maybe just getting drunk and putting myself in danger is enough to see whose side Beckett and the rest of the Retribution Kings are on.

———

A bonfire warms the cool air near the lake. It's windy out tonight even though it's early summer; the summer heat and humidity hasn't hit the city yet. In a few more weeks, a bonfire like this will feel sweltering. But for now, it lights the night sky and proves a treacherous obstacle for the drunk assholes to maneuver around.

I've been here for two hours, and no knight in shining armor has come to my rescue. Or no controlling hero with his crew of devils is more like it. Vincent's men haven't found me either. It looks like I might be on my own tonight.

I've barely drank, knowing I'll need my wits about me if they do show up. But now that I know they aren't, I decide to enjoy my night of wild freedom.

I grab two solo cups filled with beer and make my way to the crowd dancing in the firelight. I down the first cup and then sip the other while I dance. My hips sway, my arms raise over my head, and my eyes close as I let myself feel the music.

Warm bodies surround me, but I don't open my eyes, not even when grabby hands slide over my hips and sway with me. I let myself be free. Vincent thinks he can control me with threats. He thinks he can prevent me from fucking every man in the city. I may have failed at getting Beckett or the Retribution Kings to come to me, but I can piss off Vincent by fucking a guy of my choice tonight in the woods.

Another pair of hands grip my waist from the front, and I feel a hard body press against mine.

I open my eyes to see a gorgeous man in front of me— hazel eyes, cropped brown hair, and a jawline that could cut glass. I'm entranced already, not to mention the muscles I feel beneath his clothes as he pushes up against me.

I reach back as I look up at the hard man behind me. His hair is shaggier, unkempt; tattoos peek out beneath his clothes, reminding me of too many guys I had hoped were my friends.

I let my eyes grow heavy with lust as I turn from one guy to the other. I don't care which of these studs takes me to the woods and fucks me against a tree. I don't care which one makes me forget the pain and anger building in my chest, begging for a release. I just need one, or both, of them to fuck me—now.

I drain the rest of my beer and lick my lips, looking from one to the other. The front guy's mouth drops, and I'm pretty sure he's drooling. The guy behind me brushes my hair off my neck and breathes against my bare skin. This is moving far too slow for my liking.

"I'm going into the woods, and one or both of you can follow me if you dare. But I expect to be fucked so hard that I won't be able to walk straight tomorrow. If you aren't up for the challenge, don't follow me."

I shove at the guy in front while whipping the guy behind me with my long hair. And then I strut toward the woods, letting my ass sway, knowing they're staring.

I don't stop on the edge of the campsite, where I can hear many other couples moaning just at the edge of darkness. No, I keep walking five minutes into the woods, wanting to get away from the crowd. I need to scream without fear of others hearing me.

The crunch of the leaves and sticks is my only indication that the guys are following me—both by the frequency of the sound.

I grin, biting my bottom lip. Sex is one of the only

things I can control that is a big 'fuck you' to Vincent. It's also incredibly fun.

I stop walking when I feel like I've gone far enough and turn to face my followers. I'm hoping my intoxication level will make up for any lack of skills these guys have.

My eyes wide when I turn. "You brought some friends." I keep my voice level and calm as I stare at six guys.

This isn't what I signed up for. Two guys I can handle, six means giving up control completely. It means they can overpower me and do whatever they want to me. As much as I enjoyed fucking the four Retribution Kings at once, this is different. I don't know these guys. I don't trust them like I did Caius and his crew.

I fold my arms and stick out my hip, my eyes flickering on bored. "You don't all get to fuck me. I invited these two. The rest of you, get lost." I point to the two I want to fuck.

"Oh, come on, beautiful. You're a wild thing. Don't act like you don't want us all."

The guys all start taking steps toward me.

My heart thunders, and I try to clear the alcohol from my head, to think of a way out of this. I don't want to be gang-raped by a bunch of rich college pricks that think they own the world. They are just as mad as the criminals I've been running from, but at least the gangs don't try to pretend they are good like these college douchebags.

I take a step back, trying to keep my distance. I'm going to have to run and hope they are all as drunk as me and will give up the chase quickly.

A couple of guys smirk, others' eyes darken as if hunting their prey. And others stare blankly, not giving away any emotions.

"Run, baby, we like to chase," the guy closest to me says.

I run.

I can't see where I'm going, and I should run toward the bonfire, toward people who could help me. But the boys are in the way, so I don't have a choice but to run deeper into the dark woods.

I can't run full out as the ground is uneven and full of sticks, broken logs, and stumps. In the dark, I can barely see more than a couple of feet in front of me.

I can hear the boys chasing behind, growing closer with each step.

I consider pulling out my phone to call Lucy. It will attract Vincent. I don't want to go back to him, but I'd rather be locked up in his tower than raped by six men. But if I pull my phone out, it will only slow me down. Plus, I'm a solid hour away from the city; they wouldn't make it in time to save me.

My foot catches in a tree root, and I fall face-first into the ground. I immediately jump back to my feet, but it's too late. A hand grabs my arm and yanks me to his hard body.

Hoops and hollers leave the other boys, like they just caught their prey—me.

The guy's arm goes around my neck, but he doesn't bother restraining my arms. Too cocky, too convinced he has control over me.

I don't have time. I have to make a move now before the other boys grab ahold of me. I might be able to take this guy, but not six.

Instinct takes over—I bite his arm at the same time I elbow him hard in the groin.

He releases me, and I run. I don't make it ten steps before a hand grabs onto the collar of my shirt.

"Let me go, you bastard!"

"And here I thought you wanted me to play hero."

"Beckett?"

He shoves me back like he can't stand to touch me for even a second. I bounce into Caius's arms—I can't tell if he's holding me because he cares about me or because I'm their captive. Gage, Hayes, and Lennox—I spot them all in the shadows on either side of him.

"You caught her," the leader of the bro pack says with a smile. "We'll let you have her after we're done."

Beckett growls in response. "She's not yours. She's *ours.*"

"But—"

Beckett takes one step toward them, the growl still reverberating through the forest. But there must be something else in his eyes or his stance that causes the frat boys to turn around and leave us alone in the woods.

They came.

My eyes dance between each of them, trying to read their emotions, but it's like they've all turned them off. Beckett's back is still to me. I can't see Caius without turning my head and making it obvious that I'm looking for some reassurance that he still cares. Hayes won't look at me. Gage is stone. And even Lennox, who usually has his angry scowl on his face, just stares into the darkness.

Beckett turns, ignoring me completely as he starts stomping in the other direction toward a clearing.

"I'm sorry," I say.

He stops and sucks all the oxygen in the forest right along with him.

"I'm sorry about Odette. I can't imagine what it feels like to lose your wife." I look to Caius, who is still gripping my arm. "To lose your sister." I look to the other guys. "Your friend. I'm so sorry for your loss."

Beckett's head snaps toward me. His nostrils flare, and the moonlight catches his eyes, making him look possessed. Last time I saw him, he was mourning; now he's full of uncontrolled rage. It's the only thing keeping him going—holding onto his fury.

He doesn't speak. Caius releases my arm without a word and steps back with the others. It's clear they are going to let Beckett do all the talking. They are just here to support him.

Silence stretches between Beckett and me. The only thing we can hear are voices of the party in the distance.

"I'm sorry for your loss," I say again to break the silence.

"Sorry for my loss?" he chuckles. "Sorry? Why would you be sorry when you helped Corsi do it?"

"Vincent didn't kill her."

I feel the glares of the rest of the guys disagreeing with me.

"I don't want to hear your lies!" Beckett marches toward me. The move is supposed to scare me, get me to run again, but of all the people I'm scared of, Beckett isn't one of them.

He doesn't touch me, but his breath is fire. I stare longingly at his lips, remembering the last time I kissed him. Kissing him was different than any kiss I've ever had before. His kisses made me come alive; they made me feel like me, instead of whatever this version is of me.

"Corsi really did a number on you, didn't he?" he says.

I frown, my eyes narrow as I try to understand his words.

"You're so fucked up that I threaten you and all you want to do is kiss me." His hand runs up and down my hip, and I purr. "You want me to fuck you so badly. I bet your panties are soaked, am I right?"

I swallow hard, my throat tightening. My cheeks flush, but I don't look at the other guys.

He chuckles. "Pretty fucked up that you want to fuck a guy whose wife you just killed."

"I didn't kill her. I had nothing to do with her death."

"You can't even remember."

"Thanks to you all drugging me!"

He smirks.

The guys chuckle.

"You care." I narrow my eyes at him. "You wouldn't have followed me and saved me if you didn't care."

He leans in, the scruff of his facial hair scraping across my cheek. "I care...about retribution."

I shiver at his words.

"I'm not afraid of you."

"You should be."

"I want to help you."

He looks away, almost bored, ready to tell his guys it's time to go. "We already established that you can't. You don't remember anything worthwhile. But when I figure out the truth—if you had anything to do with Odette being taken or killed, you'll pay. I won't spare you."

"My memories are coming back. The fog from the drugs is slowly leaving."

He slowly turns and looks at me again.

"The guy I was running from—I remember his eyes. They're dark gray. Vincent has brown eyes. I haven't found any of his men with gray eyes yet, but I will. My memories will keep coming back."

Beckett doesn't speak.

"I can help you. I want to help you get revenge for what happened to Odette. I can find out things from Vincent, from the other guys that you can't."

"So you'll be my spy?"

I nod, looking to the others. Gage and Caius seem intrigued. Hayes seems cautious. And Lennox looks like he wants to kill me.

"And what do you want from me in return?"

"I want you to protect me when you can. Protect me, and I'll give you information. But more importantly, I want you to win the game."

Beckett cocks his head, his eyes turning to ice. "I save you, Princess, and you'll get me info? I thought you didn't want to be saved."

"I don't, but I realized that I'm vastly outnumbered. If I want to survive, I'm going to need allies."

"I save you, and you'll owe me *anything*."

I don't blink at the change of our agreement from getting him information to owing him anything he wants. It's not exactly the easy alliance I had hoped for, but he's here. He's talking to me. He wouldn't be if he didn't care.

I nod. "Every time you save me, I'll owe you whatever you want. I'll help you win the game for free, though."

He shakes his head slowly. "Oh, I plan on winning, Princess. But not so I can have the pleasure of calling you 'wife.'" He steps into my space, backing me up until he has me boxed in between him and the trunk of a large tree.

"I'm going to own you, Princess. When I win, I'll enjoy taking everything from you. Your father. Your family. Your friends. Your money. And then, eventually, your life. You'll belong to *me*."

His pain rattles through me. I welcome it if it means I can take a little of his agony away. I don't know what connection we share that makes me want to help him so much.

I know he felt a deep connection to Odette—that he should have had an eternity with her. But I can't help but feel it should have been me. We were made for each other; there is something special between us.

I doubt I'll ever change his mind. Even if he wins, he won't save me. He's not my hero, and I'm not his princess. But if I can ease his grief and he can keep me out of the hands of monsters, it will be enough.

He thinks I'm responsible for Odette's death, as do the rest of the Retribution Kings. He's wrong; I'll prove it. And I'll help him end anyone who took her from him.

I don't know why I care, why I love him already. He hates me. He doesn't want me. That will never change. And yet, I love him. I know that deep in my gut. It's a love I've never felt before. The instant I met him, I loved him and knew that he'd never be mine.

I don't know if it's a romantic love or just a pulling of two souls who have been through a similar experience, but staring into Beckett's brown eyes, everything floods back into me.

Everything.

Every memory.

Every pain.

Every heartache.

I remember why...

I remember who...

I could spill everything I know right here, right now,

but Beckett would never believe me. I have to gain his trust.

And I have to protect him.

"I owe you for saving me. What do you want me to do?"

5

BECKETT

"I owe you for saving me. What do you want me to do?" Ri says.

What do I want her to do?

I want her to tell me the truth.

I want her to admit her part in Odette's death.

I want her to be punished for her sins.

I want...

Dammit, I want her to stop risking her fucking life because she thinks I'm her hero. I'm not. I'm nobody's hero. I couldn't save Odette, a woman I love; I can't save Ri, a woman I hate.

And yet, our deal proves that she trusts me. She trusts me to save her.

She shouldn't.

I don't care about her.

I never will.

Losing the love of my life ensured I never care again. Not about her. Not about the guys who have sworn their loyalty to me. Not about any woman. I can't love. I've lost that ability.

So Ri asking me what I want her to do is dangerous. My mind flutters with possibilities. Things she could do to get me information from her father or the other players. Things that could help me get retribution.

But I don't trust her. Whatever information she brings me, I would have to verify myself. That's not very useful.

Right now, all I want to do is punish her for dragging me out of bed in the middle of the night, chasing her ass to the middle of the woods, watching her dance across a bonfire with a bunch of drunk assholes, and then watching her shake her ass and croon her finger for the guys to follow her, only for her to have gotten herself into a situation she couldn't handle.

"Do you want me to spy on Vincent? Get close to one of the other guys? Ask the guards some questions?"

"No."

She frowns, thinking I no longer want any part of our deal.

Good, let her squirm.

In the meantime, my eyes wander to the other guys I've almost forgotten are here. They all look at her with anger in their eyes, even though I know Hayes and Gage aren't upset with her. Lennox is always upset with her. And Caius—I have no clue what's going on with him. I don't know why he entered the game. *Does he want Ri or want to hurt her like me?*

Either way, it doesn't matter. I want her to suffer for what she did. I want her to realize how stupid coming here was.

"On your knees," I say.

She blinks at me. Even in the dark, I can see her shock. "What?"

"You heard me."

"Why?"

"I saved you. You owe me—*anything.*"

Her eyes lust when I say anything, and I know what she thinks I'm going to have her do. She kneels almost immediately then, begging to touch my body. She's that desperate. It's pathetic really.

With Ri on her knees, her eyes are eye level with my crotch and growing with need. She licks her lips, wanting in my pants.

I chuckle. "So eager."

The guys laugh with me. It's then that Ri remembers the other guys are still here. Slowly, she looks around as her cheeks pinken. She tucks her wavy hair behind her ear as she scans each guy and then finally returns her vision to me.

I quirk an eyebrow. "A deal's a deal."

Her throat bobs, and she slowly reaches for my pants. Fighting the urge to rip my pants down and take me hungrily like she wants, while being embarrassed that we have an audience.

I wait until she has my pants undone to stop her. I grab her wrist and pull her back.

"You think I want you to suck me off? You'd like that too much."

She sits back on her heels. "Then what do you want?"

"I want your embarrassment. I want your pain. I want your suffering. I want you to feel a hundredth of the pain you caused me!"

She flenches at my words.

My breathing is hard and uncontrollable. I feel myself losing control.

"Okay," her small voice cuts through my pain. "How do I do that?"

"Beg for what you want."

"I don't understand." She purses her lips, trying to keep her breathing steady.

"I don't trust you. We don't trust you. Maybe someday, that will change. But for now, I don't trust any information you give me. Now, all I want is for you to suffer."

"What if I'm telling the truth? What if I had nothing to do with Odette's death? You'll punish me for something I didn't do." Her eyes are fire, her words pure strength. It's going to take a lot to break her. She's not easily broken, but I'm going to enjoy every second of her pain.

"I'm not punishing you for killing Odette. If I find out you had a role, you'll know—the pain I'll inflict will be nothing compared to now."

"Then why punish me now?"

"Because you're a careless, spoiled little princess who needs to understand that we aren't at your beck and call. We aren't your heroes. I'm not your hero. And if you want to be part of our group, you have to earn my trust."

She nods softly.

"Now beg for what you want."

Her eyes dart back one more time to Caius, Hayes, Gage, and Lennox as she takes a deep, steadying breath. And then her dark eyes look up at me, hooded with lust and desire.

"Please," her voice is breathy.

I give her an amused grin. "Please? That's all you got, Princess?"

"Please, I want you. I want to suck your cock." Her cheeks are crimson. I relish her embarrassment. I stroke her long hair.

"Sorry, Princess, you don't get my cock. You haven't earned it. And I doubt you ever will." Thank god it's dark because as much as I hate her, my dick still thinks she's hot as fuck on her knees in front of me, her long eyelashes batting up at me and begging for my cock.

With her in this position, I can't completely deny myself some pleasure.

"Suck my fingers like you want my cock."

Her tongue swipes over her bottom lip, and a drop of drool drips out of the corner of lips, just thinking about it. She's desperate for me.

Ri reaches out and grabs my hand, her breathing short and nervous as she moves my hand toward her mouth. As much as she wants to touch me, any part of me, she hesitates and looks back again at our audience.

"What's wrong, Princess? They've already seen you naked. Kissed your lips. Fondled your breasts. Thrusted their cocks inside your cunt. But this is what gets you bashful?"

My words get the feisty fire to return to her eyes. My opponent returns to her true form as she grabs two of my fingers and slides them between her lips.

I don't let myself react. This isn't about my pleasure; it's about making her suffer. It appears embarrassing her is the way to do that—not physical pain, but mental. My cock doesn't get the message, though. My boxers tighten as her lips slip over my fingers, pretending they're my cock.

Her eyes lock on mine as she pumps her lips over my fingers.

I smirk at her, letting her know she's not affecting me, but I know I'm affecting her. She has no control. No power. If she wants my help, she has to be completely at my mercy.

She goes to pull her lips away, thinking she's done, but her humiliation has barely started.

"More."

Her chest heaves, and this time when she sucks my fingers into her mouth, she doesn't hold back. She pushes my fingers deep into my mouth, her tongue swirling around as she gags on my fingers. Drool slips from the corner of her mouth, and I see uncontrolled desire in her eyes.

She shuts her eyes, blocking me out, not letting me see how much this act is turning her on.

"Open your eyes, Princess."

She does, reluctantly, but that drives her to suck me harder until I let out the smallest of gasps. She gained a tiny bit of her power back. I won't let her keep it.

"Open wide," I command.

Her eyes narrow as she opens her mouth wider. I remove my fingers from her throat to button my pants, reach into my pocket, and pull out another small tracker to replace the one that I'm sure is about to exit her system.

"Stick out your tongue."

She does, her saliva dripping down her chin as she waits to see what I'm going to do.

I place the pill-like tracker on her tongue.

"Swallow."

Her eyes grow curious as she swallows, the tracker slithering down her throat.

"Good, stupid girl. Do you know how careless it was to come here to the middle of nowhere?"

She flinches.

"You're lucky your other tracker hasn't left your system yet. Lucky that we were curious enough to follow you."

"I know."

"I don't think you do." My eyes darken. "You could have been raped by a half dozen drunk college assholes."

"I could have handled it."

"Could you? You can barely handle the shame now."

She glares up at me, still on her knees.

"You say you came here because you wanted an alliance, someone who could help you during your father's twisted game. But what I really think is you're a horny, manipulative princess who is desperate for my cock before she agrees with her father to be married off."

"I'm not working with Vincent. I'm telling the truth. I came here because I care about you, all of you. And as much as I wish I was strong enough to defeat Vincent and save myself, I'm not."

"So you don't want my cock?"

She looks at me with defiance in her eyes. "No."

"Oh, really? Then you aren't soaking wet at the thought? Sucking my fingers, imagining they were my cock didn't make you hot with desire?"

She shakes her head.

"Prove it."

She undoes her pants and then slips her fingers inside her panties. Her face turns from defiant to shock as she realizes the truth. She doesn't know what to do.

I grab her arm and gently pull her hand up until I can smell her scent on her fingers.

"Liar."

She jerks her hand out of my grasp, redoes her pants, and quickly scrambles to her feet.

"I didn't—"

I put my fingers up to her lips. "You did. You lied. I don't trust you. We have a deal because I enjoy torturing you, and maybe someday you'll prove useful, but it's not because I'm your hero. It's not because I care about you. And I sure as hell won't be fucking you."

I look to the guys. "Let's go."

They all turn, and we start walking through the woods. Ri walks behind us. It takes us twenty minutes to make it back to the cars we came in. Caius, Hayes, and Gage climb into one. Lennox into the driver's seat of the other. I head to the passenger's seat, and Ri heads to the backseat when she says, "You're a liar too."

"I haven't lied."

"You lied when you said you won't be fucking me and when you said you don't care. You're not ready yet to move on; I get that. Your grief is going to take a long time to get over. But someday, you'll move on—with me or someone else. We both know it'll be me. Whether to win me and punish Vincent or because you just want me. You're going to fuck me in every sense of the word. Whether it's out of love or hate is yet to be decided. But don't lie and say you don't care about me. You wouldn't have followed me; you wouldn't have saved me, if you didn't care, Hero."

And then she climbs in the back of the car.

I want to argue with her. I want to tell her how fucking wrong she is. But the strain against the zipper of my jeans tells me she's right. I'll only hold off fucking her for so long. I may be mourning, but I'm also in desperate need of a release.

You do care, Odette's voice haunts me.

I don't.

You do.

I climb into the passenger seat, trying to ignore Odette's voice. The voice that has kept me on the path of good for so long. Now that she's gone, there is nothing to be good for, not anymore.

I don't care about Ri. I just want to make sure I dole out the correct punishment for her. If she was naive and stupid, then embarrassing her and playing with her is enough. If she was involved in Odette's death, though, she's going to wish that her father marries her off to a dangerous man who will protect her before I get my hands on her. Because there is no man more dangerous than me now.

6

———

RI

BECKETT IGNORES me as Lennox drives, I assume driving me back to Vincent. I always knew I would have to go back; I just wanted to know who my allies were. Beckett can pretend he's not on my side all he wants, but it's not the truth. He's on my side. He cares.

He can pretend he's a monster all he wants, but it's just his grief talking. I've seen his heart. I know who he is.

I need his help to survive the games, to not end up married to one of the bad guys. In return, I'll do more than just help him get retribution. I want to show him that he can live again, if not love again. There is life after his grief, no matter how hard it is.

I stare out the window as we drive, thinking about what just happened. My mind is flooded with how degrading it felt to kneel in front of him, sucking his fingers like they were his cock, and showing him how much I liked it, how much I want him.

I know my infatuation with him is ridiculous. I shouldn't want him, not like I do, but I can't help my feelings. I want a choice in my destiny, even if I don't have a

57

choice in my husband. I want to be able to choose him if only for a night, but I'm not sure he'll ever choose me back.

Lennox looks at me through the rearview mirror, his eyes judging me.

I close mine to block him out. I don't know why I felt so embarrassed, but somehow Beckett knew I would be. He knew that would be one of my weaknesses, and yet I enjoyed it—every debasing second of it. Beckett enjoyed it, too, although he will never admit it. I saw the proof in his crotch.

The car stops, and I open my eyes. We are parked outside Vincent's building.

"Ready to back out of our deal yet?" Beckett asks.

I open the door as I smirk at him. "No, our deal is still on. You save me, and I owe you anything you want. And don't think I didn't notice how bad you wanted me earlier."

Then I slam the door shut and walk inside Vincent's building.

I calm my breathing as I head up the elevator that automatically moves as I step on. No doubt that Vincent's team is monitoring the elevators.

When the doors open into Vincent's apartment, there are two new guards standing there. They flank me as I step inside, ensuring I don't run.

Vincent is standing at the entrance of the living room, waiting for my return.

"It seems I owe the Retribution Kings double now for returning you safely to me."

"It seems you do."

"Adrian and Georgio are your guards now. We'll see if they are up to the challenge of watching you."

"What happened to Dario and Leone?"

"They've been punished for losing you."

"Punished how?" I ask cautiously.

"Bullet to the head. They fucked up; they knew the consequences."

I swallow down vile. Two men died because of me.

"And how are you going to punish me?"

"I don't punish you, Rialta. We make deals. We have agreements. I protect you no matter how hard you fight me. I let you live your life as long as you are safe."

Two dangerous men. Two dangerous games. And I'm not sure I'm strong enough to win both of them.

"So I'm free to go?"

"If you want. But the guards go with you."

I frown. I don't want the guards anywhere near Lucy. And I'm not ready to have more blood on my hands if I slip away on their watch.

"Get some sleep, Rialta. Tomorrow the first round of games begins."

———

A gown is laid out for me the next evening, along with another fucking tiara. I stuck to my room for most of the day. I should have been searching Vincent's house for anything that might help Beckett find out who killed Odette, but I didn't. Beckett doesn't trust me yet, even if I did find something.

The gown is beautiful, but Vincent made it clear that he isn't going to punish me. It may only be a small act of defiance, but I don't put on the sleek shiny silver gown that Adrian brought in. Instead, I head into the closet.

I don't know why tonight is another black-tie affair if

it's supposed to be a competition to the death for me. Or if Vincent just expects me to be dressed up to watch a brawl. I'm the prize, after all.

I won't let him forget that I entered the game too. I'm competing for myself as much as anyone else. I want to be able to choose if or when I marry.

I already know my closet is filled with beautiful dresses; any one would do for tonight. I let my hand trace over the silk, satin, and lace fabrics—dresses I've worn to countless different events. I like wearing dresses; they make me feel radiant and powerful. Who knew that the right dress and killer heels could wield as much power as a sword.

But that won't be what I wear tonight. I have no idea what to expect, but I'm going to be as prepared as any of the guys. Even if they are in tuxes, if I were to wear a tight dress, they'd be at an advantage for anything physical.

Who am I kidding? They will always be at an advantage if the competition is purely physical.

I walk to the back of the large walk-in closet, which is bigger than my bedroom at the apartment I share with Lucy. I find a pair of black slacks, a sparkly tank top, and a black jacket—perfect. Still formal, but something I can actually move in.

In the bathroom, I get dressed quickly, put on minimal makeup, and fix my hair in a high bun. I head back into the closet to find shoes. I scan the floor—heels, heels, 6-inch heels, tiny spiked heels no one can walk in.

There has to be something that's not a heel. While I could use my heels as a weapon, they aren't great for running or much else. But I find nothing but spiky heels. I slip on the shortest pair I can find that still has me towering, and then I walk out.

Adrian and Georgio are looking at me. Georgio has the audacity to raise his eyebrows.

"I wouldn't judge if I were you. The last guy that did I had killed," I say, strutting out of my bedroom and down the stairs.

I don't get any more looks or attitude from either of them, as we all head down the elevator to the waiting limo in silence.

Georgio holds the back door open for me.

I duck my head in and find the backseat empty. "Where's Vincent?"

"He's meeting us there. He had business he had to attend to first."

"Who did he have to kill this time?" I ask, under my breath.

"Stephan," Georgio says.

I cock my head, staring at Georgio until I realize he's serious.

I sigh and climb into the backseat. I'm never going to escape the killings. My heart doesn't race, though; I don't get anxiety or fear thinking about it. Maybe I'm more used to it than I want to admit.

———

We don't head to the same ballroom as before. This time, we head to a skyscraper and up to the top floor. When you're the head of the mafia, you can never be too careful. Never go to the same place twice. Always demand respect. Strike fear into your enemies and allies equally. And be generous when you pay someone off. Guessing by the extravagant bar and security measures in the place that Vincent rented out, he paid off the owner very well.

I don't get any time to take in my surroundings though, I have thirty-plus pairs of eyeballs on me, staring at me like they own me. I have to make them realize they don't. Even if they win and Vincent forces me to marry them, I'll never be theirs. I'll never obey, never be property. They should give up now before they risk their death for nothing.

It's hard to convey that with a single look or walk, but I put every ounce of confidence and self-ownership into my strut. I hold my head up high, and for a moment, I'm thankful for my heels that elevate me eye to eye with most of the men.

Apparently, my walk isn't good enough because one of the guys catcalls me, which causes the rest to follow suit.

I spot Caius out of the corner of my eye. He looks like he's about to murder a dozen men with one punch. Beckett is standing next to him in a sharp tux, just like every other man here, but Beckett looks stronger than them all. It's not just because he's rolled the right sleeve up to accommodate his missing limb, but because, unlike every other man here, he doesn't react.

He doesn't show his emotions on the surface. He doesn't act like a horny bastard whistling my name, nor is he boiling like Caius. He's just staring at me, waiting for me to decide what to do. He raises one eyebrow, and I know with one nod he'd step in and save me.

I almost nod just to see what he would do, but I don't. Not because I'd owe him, but because I don't want anyone defending me right now. I need to show these guys I'm capable of defending myself. Only when I can't do I want Beckett stepping in.

He seems to get the message because he just sips his drink, looking bored. I wish I could say the same about

Caius. If I don't do something soon, he's going to get himself killed. I have enough blood on my hands. His death is not something I want on my conscience. He's too good. Too kind. Too worthy.

I stop suddenly, my bodyguards almost bumping into me from behind. As much as they will physically protect me, they aren't doing much to stop the verbal harassment.

I don't really have a plan, but old strategies come to me nonetheless. I let my instincts take over.

Find an easy target.

I scan the crowd of men quickly. I find a young guy; he can't be older than eighteen, with a big mouth.

I walk toward him.

Draw him in.

I lick my bottom lip, watching him whistle louder than all the rest. I need him a little closer. I don't know why. I don't know what I'm going to do. But I give him the tiniest wink in encouragement as he steps forward and puts his hands on my waist, slipping it around to my ass as he jerks me toward him.

Bingo.

"We don't need to finish the games, guys; it seems like she's already chosen me," he says.

I don't give him any warning. I don't even process what I'm going to do until I'm doing it. But one second, his hand is on my ass; the next second, he's laid out on the floor.

The heckling stops.

Everyone is staring at me for different reasons. "I suggest you keep your hands and comments to yourself from now on." Then I walk to the other side of the room and take a seat at an empty table, while Adrian and Georgio stand behind me.

"Thanks for the help, guys," I say sarcastically.

"I don't know why the last guys got fired. You can defend yourself. All we have to do is stand here and look pretty," Adrian says.

"Killed, not fired. And it was just a lucky move. That guy was weak."

"It was skilled and practiced. You don't lay someone out like that, being as small as you are, without a lot of practice."

Hmm. I flick through my memories, trying to remember a time where I learned anything about how to defend myself. I remember getting Lucy into self-defense classes, but I don't remember taking them myself.

Vincent steps into the room, grabbing everyone's attention. Figuring out what skills I have will have to wait until later.

"It seems that everyone has finally arrived," Vincent says, staring at me intensely. I guess I might have been a little bit late. *Oops.*

I just smile like I'm not phased at all.

Vincent continues, "Thank you for meeting here on such short notice. Part of joining my family is putting loyalty and family above all others. The safety of those I love matters a great deal to me. So the time and place of each game will not be named until the last moment. If you can't arrive on time for any reason, I will assume you no longer value my family, my daughter, or my time, and you will forfeit your spot in the game."

He looks around the room, assessing everyone like he's trying to take in their attire and if it's good enough or not. He doesn't look two seconds at me, so Georgio and Adrian must have already let him know that I didn't wear the approved dress, or he doesn't care.

I spend the moment looking out the window at the

darkening sky as lights begin to twinkle from the city below us. The river cuts through the buildings next to us. It would be a beautiful bar to sit at if this wasn't just another twisted day in my life where evil men compete for me like I'm a trophy.

"Rialta, if you will come here, please," Vincent says.

The room spins toward me. For a second, I consider saying no, just to see what he'll do. *Will he punish me in front of them? Will he laugh off my disobedience?*

But then I look at his eyes. He'll hurt someone I love. He'll hurt Lucy if I don't. It doesn't seem like something worth Lucy getting hurt over, so I stand and walk to Vincent's side.

One of Vincent's men hands me the same bowl from before.

"As I told you before, I don't have the time to come up with dozens of games each time; that's your job. Coming up with an appropriate game that tests the skills needed to be part of my family is part of the game. Come up with a shitty game and you're done. I'll add my own rules, spin, and twists as necessary."

Everyone stares at Vincent as he speaks. "Now, Rialta, draw a name. That man will be responsible for choosing the first game."

"Or woman," I mumble under my breath. My name is in here too. I study Vincent's face. *Unless he removed it?*

He doesn't speak to my comment, so I have no clue. Mafia men are usually a man of their word. It's one of the reasons they are so respected. I've never seen Vincent go back on his word before. He's careful with his words. You have to be careful when you make a deal with him to get what you want from him, but you don't have to worry about him going back on a deal—my name is in the bowl.

I take a deep breath, hoping I can draw my own name and somehow come up with a game that will end this nightmare. I pull a name out and read the smudged ink smeared with blood.

"Jameson Lory."

The man steps forward with excitement in his blue eyes. He runs his hand through his blonde hair with a goofy grin as several men pat his back in congratulations.

I resist the urge to look at Beckett or Caius. I need to feel Vincent out this first game. I don't want him to think I favor them. He'd probably disqualify them just for that reason alone.

"You have ten minutes to come up with a game," Vincent says.

"I don't need ten minutes," the foolish boy says.

"Well, what will it be then?" Vincent says, his jaw ticking just slightly. I doubt anyone else notices, but it's already a strike against the boy.

"If we are to be her husband, we should be able to please her."

Oh, no. Is he going to suggest touching me, fucking me, raping me already?

Vincent looks pleased by this turn of events.

"Whoever is the best kisser, according to Rialta, wins."

I grin on the outside. Yes, kissing thirty devils seems like a horrible way to spend my evening, but it's better than being touched. And he gave me power. I get to decide who wins. But it won't be a game that Vincent likes.

He stares at the boy, who just sealed his fate.

"What specifically are the rules?"

"Five minutes alone with her. You can't remove clothing. You can only touch her with your lips. She ranks us all."

Vincent looks bored now. "You can use the room there." He motions to a small, almost closet-sized room, surrounded by translucent glass where I'm sure exotic dancers press against when they dance. "And I'll add one small rule—whoever can make her scream the loudest with just their mouth wins an automatic ticket to the next round."

I'm surprised Vincent is going to accept this guy's idiotic game, but maybe he's already over this contest to care. He gets what he wants—control over the different gangs and others threatening his power. And in the end, he gets to choose the most powerful alliance.

I have power in this game. I can scream when Beckett or Caius kiss me if I want them to advance. I can choose them as the best kisser. I can rank those I'm afraid of lower.

Hungry eyes from every angle twist the acid in my stomach.

It's just a kiss—thirty-three kisses, to be exact.

My stomach burns at the thought, but I refuse to throw up. I refuse to show disgust, fear, anything.

I glance at Vincent out of the corner of my eye. He stares at me expectantly. And I remember—he's been preparing me for this all my life. I remember the rules. They have five minutes to kiss me. They can only use their lips. But no one said anything about me having to let them kiss me. No one said anything about fighting back.

I'm ready.

BECKETT

I ROLL my eyes at the ridiculous game the boy came up with. He looks maybe nineteen, practically the same age as Ri. And while I often think of her decisions as immature and irrational, his game is beyond foolish. He'll end up paying the price for it. I can see it in Corsi's eyes. The boy won't be winning this game. He'll be lucky to make it out of here unscathed.

I glance around at the at least a dozen boys that I hope learn from him. They have no business being in this game. They may be the same age as Ri, but they have no way of winning. Not when there are skilled monsters prowling, looking for their ticket to a mafia kingdom.

"Jameson will go first. Then names will be drawn to determine the order after that," Corsi says, his tone deep and menacing.

Jameson smiles and practically skips toward the glass box while some smile and lick their lips at the thought of getting to make out with the princess. Others snicker, but the smart ones stand idly by knowing these first few games are just ways to weed out the idiots from the serious players.

Corsi whispers something in Ri's ear. She doesn't react to his words, but I'm guessing he's giving her orders. I just can't tell if she's a willing participant or if she's truly trapped in this world.

A moment later, she's walking toward the box. Her shoulders are back, causing her breasts to push out against the thin material of her sparkly top that dips low enough to show her ample cleavage. Her tight pants hug the curve of her ass and the taut muscles of her thighs. Her heels clank against the floor as everyone stares, formulating a plan for how they are going to win her and the empire that comes with her.

Everyone here has their own reasons for wanting her, and I'm going to figure them all out.

Ri's bodyguards follow her as she approaches the glass box. One holds out his hand to her to help her climb up the three steps that lead into the box. She refuses his hand, climbing effortlessly up in her spiked heels. She steps into the box that is no more than three feet by three feet, leaving only a foot of space between her and Jameson.

A guard standing next to Corsi opens his phone; I'm guessing to start a timer.

The boy grins and says something to Ri that none of us can hear.

A vicious smile slinks up her lips as she crosses her arms across her chest, her hip jutting out. She's going to destroy him. He has no idea who she is. Yes, Ri is a princess, one who has never been given power over her own life, but she's also damn strong. She's no pushover. I don't know why she does what Corsi says. I don't know why she stays when she could run. But she doesn't follow orders unless she wants to.

Jameson steps close, going in for a kiss.

She slaps him hard across the cheek, loud enough that we all hear her hand make contact with his face.

Ooohs, ahhhs, and chuckles leave the crowd.

Jameson grabs his cheek as shock and embarrassment flash in his eyes.

"Stupid boy didn't realize that he needed to specify all the rules. He never made any rules for Ri. She can make this as hard as she wants for us. All we can use is our mouth to fight back. She's going to annihilate all of us," Caius says from next to me.

I lift my drink to my mouth. "Probably. At least the weak."

"She'll let us kiss her, though," he says.

He's probably right about that too, but I don't care about the damn kissing game. I have more important things to do.

I tear my eyes from the glass box as Jameson tries a running approach that she easily sidesteps. He'll be lucky if he gets his lips anywhere near her and is able to leave without a black eye.

I turn my attention to Corsi, whose lips turn up just the slightest as he watches his daughter. He seems proud, which only strengthens my resolve that she's working with him.

"Oooh, that's got to hurt," a guy to our left says, watching the show.

I ignore him, despite my urge to see what Ri did. I saw what she did to him earlier.

I still can't figure her out. *Is she trained or just full of rage?*

"So, what's your plan for kissing her, Beckett?" Hayes asks in my ear.

"My plan is to observe the others and figure out the serious players. My plan is to listen in on conversations, to approach people and see how they react to me, see if they have a vendetta against me or us. My plan is to see if I recognize anyone. My plan is to place tracking and listening devices on anyone I can. That's my plan. It doesn't matter if I kiss her or not."

"Fair enough," Hayes chuckles; he can't resist stirring up trouble. "Caius?"

"I'm going to kiss her like she's never been kissed, make her want me," he says stone-faced, still watching Jameson's attempt to kiss her.

"And what if she was involved in Odette's death?" I ask.

"Then, it will hurt her worse if she has feelings for me when we end her."

My eyes search his, but all I see is the truth. Still no grief, just stillness and truth.

"Damn, she's kicking his ass," comes Lennox from my ear. "And I was hoping to get to watch her disgust as she gets kissed over and over again. But I bet no one other than ones she wants to kiss get anywhere near her."

"Why do you hate her so much anyway?" Hayes asks.

"Besides the fact that I think she's been lying to us this whole time? She's Corsi's daughter. She grew up with him, shares his blood. Some of him is bound to rub off on her," Lennox says, the anger in his voice hiding his pain. This is personal; Corsi hurt someone he cared about.

I hear a smack, and then Hayes grumbles. "Jesus, Gage, what was that for?"

"For being an idiot. You know why Lennox feels the way he does. Now, stop gabbing and let Beckett and Caius focus. You should focus on her guards, the guy on your left is staring at Corsi more than Ri, and the taller guy behind you has been staring at you two," Gage says. He hacked into the security feed and has been watching the whole scene on his phone.

"I'll take the guy behind us; you take the guy on our left," I say to Caius.

He nods.

And then we split up. My target is a tall, handsome man with dark, harsh eyes. His gaze doesn't shift from me as I walk in his direction. He makes no move to hide his attention, which is going to make it hard to tag him with a listening and tracking device without him knowing what I'm doing.

I'm used to being stared at, but this guy isn't staring because of my arm. I take in his dark hair, sharp eyes, the scar on his cheek, but none of it rings a bell. I don't know this man. I don't know why he would target me or Odette.

But I won't forget his face.

I down my drink. There is a bar behind him, so I make that my mission as I pass, avoiding his stare. I target one of his buddies instead, slapping a tiny device Gage gave me on the back of his jacket before I walk to the bar and order another drink.

The bartender immediately slides another scotch my way. She's been keeping the drinks flowing; it's easier for Corsi to control us that way. I take my drink and turn my attention back to the box.

"Time," the guard next to Corsi says.

One of Ri's guards opens the door and escorts a bloodied-nose Jameson out of the box.

She drew blood—impressive.

The guard calls out another name, and a guy to my left

removes his jacket and rolls up his sleeves like he's about to enter a boxing ring instead of a tiny glass box with a girl he's supposed to kiss. He has muscles where the boy had none. Thick biceps, buff shoulders—not that he can use his muscles to grab her. But he's far more intimidating than the boy. I'm curious if she fights him off or if he gets a kiss in.

He walks into the box cautiously, like he's approaching a lion.

Ri's removed her jacket, her strong shoulders ready as she holds up her fists in front of her face.

He licks his bottom lip, his eyes roaming over her body. He takes a step, trying to box her in, giving her little space to throw her arm back to get a punch in. She takes a step back before she realizes her mistake. He pushes his head quickly between her fists, and his lips land hard against hers.

"Well, that didn't last long," Lennox says giddily.

The man is good-looking, strong, and smart. And the way he moves his mouth over hers is skilled. She can't help but enjoy his kiss.

I figure she's given up fighting him and turn my eyes away to study the room when there's a collective gasp then chuckle. My eyes glance back to see the man on his ass and her smirking triumphantly over him.

"You owe me fifty bucks, Len," Hayes says through my earpiece.

"I'll regain it soon enough. She can't keep this up. She's not strong enough or in good enough shape to take down thirty guys. Just hope your names are drawn last, and she'll be too tired to put up much of a fight," Lennox says.

I hold my glass up to cover my mouth, so no one sees me talking to myself. "You don't have to worry about us.

She wants us both. I'm sure it's why she and her father killed Odette, so that she could marry one of us instead. They want the Retribution Kings for their own," I say, afraid that by coming up with this game, I played right into their hands. I gave Corsi a way to chose Caius or me as her husband without ruining his alliances with the rest.

I glance to Corsi, who is staring at me like he's already won. He doesn't know what I have planned for him. I just need proof that I'm right.

I sit at the bar while Gage reports the conversations of the two guys we've put the listening devices on, but it's mostly nothing. Hopefully, when they return home, they will be more open with their motives.

Guys enter and leave the box with Ri. Most don't get their lips near her. Some achieve a few seconds kiss. The longest was about ten seconds. No one has managed to make her scream. And Ri holds them all off in different ways.

Caius approaches me.

"She's been trained. She knows all the most sensitive places to attack. She varies her attacks so no one can predict what she's going to do next. After twenty guys, she's barely breaking a sweat," Caius says.

I nod my agreement and tighten my eyes. "She played us, pretending to be the damsel in distress. She was never in distress. She's been manipulating us this whole time."

Caius narrows his eyes. "Maybe, but I want proof before we hurt her. We need her to trust us."

"You get her to trust you. I'll make her fear me."

"Caius Monroe," the guard calls his name out.

"Make her pay for what she did," I say.

He downs his drink. "She's going to be declaring her love for me as soon as my lips grace hers."

"Just cover your balls, bro," Hayes says from our earpieces.

"Nah, she likes me, thinks I'm sweet. She won't nail me in the balls."

"Clearly because she doesn't know you," Hayes jokes back.

Then Caius goes silent as he approaches the box. The long-haired guard opens the door for Caius, who steps in without emotion.

Ri studies him carefully.

They both stand on opposite sides of the box, about a foot of space between them. Neither of them speaks, but it doesn't seem they need to. Ri stands at the ready just like she has with every other man—she won't let him near her without him getting a black eye, knocked on his ass, or a kick to the groin.

I lift my drink as I watch closely. Maybe getting his ass kicked will knock some emotion into Caius.

Caius leans against the glass door casually, like he doesn't care about what happens next. His mouth moves, and I know he's speaking, but I can't read lips, and he must have turned off his microphone.

I glance to Ri, ready to see her mind race with devious ways she plans on taking Caius down just like the rest of them. Her mind is working alright, but instead of thinking how she's going to pummel his ass, her teeth scrape over her bottom lip. Her eyes glaze with whatever dirty thoughts he's planting in her head.

Whatever he's saying, Caius is good. He's going to win by just spewing poetic, sweet nothings in her ear.

He takes a step, slow but purposeful, toward her.

Her hand that has been fisted, ready to throw a punch, relaxes. She doesn't even notice when he takes another step, encroaching on her personal space as he speaks again.

She closes her eyes, and her chest swells as she holds her breath.

He doesn't hesitate in the small opening she gives him. His lips dance over hers so slowly that I'm not even sure she realizes he's kissing her. He coaxes her mouth open, holding his tongue back until she parts her lips on her own as she sucks in a deep breath. Then he makes his move. His tongue glides inside her pink lips, and her head tilts back as he catches her breath in his throat.

I want to tear my eyes away. He's just playing her the same way I will, the same way she's played us. Watching them together is just distracting me from doing what I came here to do—gather information about all the men in this room.

But I can't tear my eyes away.

Glass breaks. I hear it before I feel it—the sticky alcohol, the sharp edges, the warm blood oozing out of the wound on my palm. I squeezed the glass I was holding so hard that it broke in my hand.

My nostrils flare, my heart races, and my chest heaves with each breath. A primal reaction grows deep in my core as I watch him kiss her like she's a princess—tenderly, sweetly, and lovingly. And she lets him. She doesn't fight. She wants him.

That's why I'm angry. He's treating her like an ally, not the enemy. I know his plan is to make her fall in love with him, but I suspect he'll be falling for her long before she falls for him.

"You okay, sir?" the bartender says from behind me.

I nod, still not looking away as the rage rolls around in my chest like a fire growing out of control.

He hands me a napkin as I drop the broken glass to the floor. I wipe my hand, removing the blood and sticky residue of alcohol.

But I wish I had another glass to shatter right now or a brick wall to punch. Caius is no longer coaxing Ri, Ri is kissing him back.

I want to tear their lips apart.

No, what I really want is to punch Caius in the face.

Thankfully, Ri finally comes to her senses and does that for me.

It's a hard punch; she throws her full body into it even though she barely has the space to draw her arm back. But it's enough to draw blood.

Caius touches his split lip, wiping the single drop of blood off. He doesn't show emotion. No cocky smirk. No triumphant smile. No shock at her outburst.

He just turns and walks out even though his time isn't over yet, leaving Ri to glare at the back of his head.

Caius makes his way to a group of men that he's supposed to be spying on after he leaves the box. He doesn't come to talk to me; he doesn't approach me at all.

The guys joke in my earpiece about the kiss and the punch, but I click the volume off. I can't hear any of it. I'm still trying to process my reaction and why I'm feeling it. My inner heat sweeps through me until my entire body is on fire. All I feel is the tingling of jealousy of another man touching what's mine.

My plaything.

My enemy.

Mine.

A couple more men are called next. None of them get close to her. Most don't try after seeing the rage in her eyes after Caius succeeded where the others didn't.

I don't understand why she's so upset. She likes Caius. *Is she just mad she let her feelings for him show so soon in front of her father, who will probably eliminate him first round just because she likes him?*

"Beckett," my name is finally called.

Now I know exactly how I'm going to make it clear to her that she belongs to me, not Caius, not her father, not any other man in this room. I may hate her, but that doesn't make it any less true.

8

RI

I'M on autopilot as I punch, kick, attack, and generally ensure that every guy that enters after Caius gets nowhere near my lips and leaves in enough pain that they won't come near me again. My mind is still on that kiss, on our conversation, on everything that happened when Caius stepped foot in this glass box.

Caius leans against the box, barely looking at me. His eyes are glossy. He shows no emotion, but I can tell he's thinking about his sister, about his loss. Beckett wasn't the only one who had his heart ripped out of his chest. While Beckett has become a tornado of rage, Caius is a calm sea. He's capable of rhythmic waves or a hurricane of emotions at any moment.

"I'm not going to let you kiss me. Not even you, Caius," I say.

"Been there, done that, right?" His eyes twinkle for just a moment with the memory of our last kiss and him fucking me.

"Something like that." I settle my racing heart, trying not to think about what we've already done together. I can't let Vincent know whom I prefer or don't. I need Caius and Beckett in this game as long as possible.

To protect me? Yes.

But also because I just need them. Both of them, for very different reasons.

"I understand where you and I stand. You want him, not me."

My eyebrows raise. He's not wrong. I want Beckett even though I should want Caius.

"You also hate him and want payback for that embarrassing little thing he made you do."

"I wasn't embarrassed."

"I saw your flushed cheeks and wide eyes."

I frown.

"Let me help you get payback. Make him jealous. Make him crazy."

"That would be impossible since Beckett doesn't care about me. He hates me. He thinks I'm responsible for Odette's death, just like you do. I can't trust either of you."

"A bet then? You seem to like bets."

He's right. I do like bets. It makes me feel in control of uncontrollable situations. It's why I have deals or bets with Vincent and Beckett.

"What are we betting? Because it seems like you are wasting an awful lot of your time talking and standing over there, when you should be over here trying to kiss me. It seems like you're scared."

"When I kiss you, if Beckett gets jealous, I win. You owe me anything I choose."

I roll my eyes as he says anything, just like Beckett did the other night.

"And when I let you kiss me, and Beckett doesn't get jealous, then I get *anything* I want."

"Deal. Now, act like what I'm saying is turning you on."

My mind immediately goes to Beckett, but I don't let it. Instead, I think about that night in the VIP room. The night that I let four men fuck me at once.

I rake my teeth over my bottom lip and let my breathing slow. My heart races until my blood is boiling with need.

I want to look to see if Beckett is watching, but I don't let myself.

Caius steps forward, and I let him. I relax my fists and remind myself not to throw a punch when his lips hit mine.

Then he kisses me.

At first, I don't kiss him back. It takes everything in me just to let him kiss me. And then something changes, and I'm kissing him back. It's sweet, nauseatingly sweet. But my toes curl, and a soft moan vibrates in my throat. It's a nice kiss. If this was any other circumstance, I would drag him back to my apartment and fuck him senseless. I would date him and enjoy the wild ride. Maybe I'd even marry him someday.

But this isn't that.

This is about my survival.

So I punch him hard with a roar of emotion. I catch his lip, and blood immediately spills.

I wait for Caius to try again. He doesn't.

He walks away like he's already gotten what he wanted from me.

It takes everything in me to not look at Beckett, to not see his reaction. I don't know which reaction I want more from him—for him to not to be jealous and for me to win the bet or for him to be jealous and lose. If he's jealous, then there's hope he could be mine, even if only for one day.

Finally, I gather the courage to look.

Beckett is looking at me like he wants to kill someone. Me, probably. Caius, definitely.

Caius won.

But I'm about to win too.

———

Beckett's name is finally called, and I'm desperate to get my victory. The vein on Beckett's forehead is bulging, there's a stain of blood on his hand, and there's fury in his eyes as he storms toward the glass cage. It all confirms what I saw across the room before—Beckett was jealous as fuck.

Why?

And why is my heart doing that little pitter-patter thing?

He hates me.

I just want to manipulate him into one night of fucking to help him realize that he can move on from Odette. That he's stronger than his loss.

Beckett steps into the box, never taking his brown eyes off of me.

The glass door shuts behind him. Just like Caius, he stands there wordlessly as time starts to tick. His hungry eyes devour me with his stare.

Inside, I shutter.

Outside, I'm solid as ice.

I won't let him embarrass me.

I won't let him win, not this time.

"You going to try to kiss me or just stand there?"

"No, I'm not going to try and kiss you."

I blink, confused.

"Then, what are you going to do?"

"I'm going to help you realize something that I thought I made perfectly clear last night."

"And what's that?"

He doesn't answer me. He steps forward. I try to step back, but there is nowhere for me to go.

The glass box is tiny, but it has never felt as suffocating as it does now with Beckett in here with me. He hasn't tried to touch me. His breath is still far enough away that I can't feel the heat. And still, my body tingles with tiny sparks of desire.

What is it about this guy that gets me instantly turned on and full of rage at the same time?

It doesn't matter that I'm equal parts lust and hate. This is going to be fun either way.

I don't let him move another inch toward me before I start throwing punches.

I know he's going to dodge the first throw, but I'm surprised when he ducks the second completely as well. I don't even graze the side of his cheek.

"You think you can hit me, Princess?"

"I don't think; I know."

I throw another punch, but again I miss as he glides effortlessly out of the way.

I don't know how he moves so smoothly in such a small space. None of the other guys moved as gracefully.

I frown, the lines in my forehead deepening into a scowl as Beckett easily anticipates every one of my moves. *Is it because we are so in tune with one another? Or is he just that much better at fighting than me?* All he can do is avoid; he can't touch me. And yet, he's beating me.

"What's wrong, Ri? I know you've been trained, but maybe you aren't as skilled as you thought."

I swing again. I miss.

He snickers. "I don't even need to fight back in order to win; that's how inexperienced you are. You can go against a punching bag all you want in a gym, but when it comes to real-life, you are woefully unprepared."

I grind my teeth together. "I beat thirty other men. I'd say that's pretty good—"

"Even if you can't beat me?" His sparkling grin infuriates me.

I swing low, aiming for his gut and hoping that if I aim for the middle of him, I'll have a better chance of hitting at least one part of him.

He moves as I do. I focus entirely on his stomach. I'm not going to miss this time.

My punch lands, not on his stomach, but right in the center of his chest, just over his heart.

His chest is hard, but I know it hits his broken heart of steel.

Before I can process that I actually hit him, his lips land on mine.

It sucks all the air from my lungs.

It steals all of my emotions.

It even stops my heart.

His kiss is the polar opposite of Caius's kiss. While that kiss was slow, gentle, sweet, this kiss is fast, harsh, and controlling.

I can't think.

I can't make a sound.

All I feel is his lips, his tongue. He's able to control every part of my body with just his lips. My heart flickers, my breathing stops, my blood circulates so fast that it feels like fire rushing through my veins.

I yield to him my thoughts, my soul, my heart. They're all his.

I never want this kiss to stop. It pushes away my demons. It calms the anxiety, the fear, the pain. It all disappears because of him.

The slickness of his tongue manipulating mine shoots straight to my core, and I feel the wetness pooling between my legs. My nipples pebble beneath my shirt. It takes all of my willpower not to wrap my legs around his waist and let him carry me out of here.

Fight back. Don't let him win.

That voice penetrates like a whisper in the wind, but it's enough to remind me that I shouldn't be letting Beckett kiss me. I shouldn't let him win.

Just as I'm about to knee him in the balls, the kiss stops, and I'm standing in darkness. It takes me a second to realize that I closed my eyes during the kiss. When I open them, Beckett is gone.

But I get his message loud and clear as my breathing finally returns—he can control me. I'm his plaything. I'm his revenge. As soon as he gets the evidence he seeks, he's going to destroy me.

Beckett is the last man to go, so as soon as the blood reenters my brain, I walk out. Adrian holds out his hand to me, and I take it, needing it to stay balanced after that wicked kiss. The blood is still slowly making its way north.

I continue to hold onto him for support as we walk over to where Vincent and his guard sit at a table nursing their drinks.

Vincent gives a curt nod to his guard. Blank stands up, pulls out his gun, and fires it straight into Jameson's heart.

He drops to the floor with a grin on his face. He didn't even have time to react to what just happened.

There isn't a sound, a protest, a reaction from the group around me. There isn't one from me either. The boy didn't deserve to die for his stupidity, but I don't mourn the loss of any man who tried to win me so he could control me like a dog.

I spot Beckett out of the corner of my eye. *Then, why did you enjoy his controlling kiss?*

Because I'm fucked up, that's why. And because behind his cruel exterior, deep down Beckett cares about those he loves. He just doesn't love me. He can never love me.

"Now that that's taken care of, let's discuss who the winner is," Vincent says like he didn't just order his guard to kill a boy for picking a stupid game.

I wait for Vincent to ask me who was the best kisser, but he never looks at me.

"Caius made her scream the loudest; therefore, he's the winner."

I gasp.

I guess, technically, I did moan the loudest with Caius when I hit him, while I was silent with Beckett, too consumed to make a sound. It doesn't really matter which one wins as long as Vincent doesn't shoot them. But I'm surprised Vincent would pick anyone that he thought I enjoyed.

"Your reward is you get her until the next competition. Your job is to keep her safe, alive, and ensure she returns for the next game. Other than that, you can do what you want with her except for one thing—you're forbidden from fucking her."

9

RI

THE DRIVE IS awkward and silent, far too silent for my liking. I consider speaking many times, but I bite my tongue every time. *What would I say?*

I'm squished in the back of a two-door Maserati coupe, sitting sideways with my legs bent and my knees still digging into the back of Beckett's seat as he speeds down the interstate. I realize we are leaving the city, not headed to either of their condos. We must be headed back to the cabin.

Caius closes his eyes in the passenger seat, somehow able to sleep despite Beckett's reckless driving and the anger rolling off of Beckett. I can't tell if his fury is directed at Caius, me, or both of us.

Beckett works his jaw; I can hear the cracking and popping of the veins in his throat. My guess is he's upset with both of us.

Caius doesn't seem phased, even if Beckett is his boss now.

I chew on my tongue until it bleeds. I just kicked thirty guys' asses, but I can't take the silence and glares from

Beckett. That's not true—he's not glaring at me. He's just blazing his fury out in all directions, and I'm too sensitive to not soak it all in.

"I—"

"I wouldn't finish your sentence, Princess," Beckett says. The way he says 'princess' is like a curse leaving his mouth.

So I shut up. I'm too exhausted to fight, even with him. But I can't sleep like Caius.

As we get closer to the cabin, Beckett seems to settle, so I spit out the words I've wanted to say this entire trip. "If it was up to me, you would have won, Hero, not Caius. His kiss whispered to my heart; yours slashed through the darkness of my soul to claim me."

"I always win, Princess. When will you stop doubting me? I didn't care about winning the stupid game. My goal was simple—ensure you know who you belong to. Have you finally figured it out? Who do you belong to?"

"The Retribution Kings," I answer.

"No, you don't belong to them. You belong to *me*. You're my retribution."

Beckett slams on the breaks and gets out of the car without another word. I stare after him.

His.

Not the Retribution Kings'.

His.

What does that mean? Does he like me? Want me?

No, he just wants to make me pay for what he thinks is my role in his wife's death.

"Caius, we're here," I say, pushing on the back of his seat.

He stirs slowly, then climbs out and moves his seat up so I can get out. He extends his hand to me—always the gentleman—and I take it. I hate having a guy help me, even with something so little, but I should get used to it. I need as much help as I can get.

I shiver when I climb out, and Caius immediately removes his tux jacket and places it over my shoulders. I'm only wearing my sparkly tank, black pants, and heels.

I take one step in my heels before Caius grabs my elbow, helping me walk the uneven terrain into the cabin. The second we reach the door, I kick my shoes off and shrug myself free from Caius. I almost wish that I hadn't, that I was still connected to Caius, my defender. Maybe then the stares of all the guys wouldn't flush my cheeks bright red.

In the last two meetings with these guys, I was getting fucked by them and then down on my knees, begging for Beckett's cock, sucking his fingers instead in the middle of the woods.

The only one not looking at me is Beckett, who has grabbed the laptop off of Gage's lap and is studying it carefully.

"So Caius is the best kisser, huh? I seem to remember you liking my kisses the best, Princess," Lennox says with a wicked smirk.

He kissed me? I just thought he held me down when they all fucked me. He hates me. *Why would he participate?*

Hayes jumps up, and before I realize what he's doing, he plants a quick kiss on my lips. "That's just because I didn't enter. If I had, she would have said I was the best kisser." He winks at me, and my fists at my side loosen just a little. I consider punching him, but then I realize it's just some leftover instinct from when I was in that box. I don't actually want to punch Hayes. The kiss was nothing.

Gage stands up next, and his arms go around me

before I realize what he's doing. My arms dangle awkwardly at my sides as Gage holds me in a hug.

"Ignore them; I can't believe you took down that many guys. You're going to have to show me what you've got later," Gage says, finally releasing me.

I still don't know what to say. All I can think about is being naked in front of them. Of them fucking me. Of me down on my knees, sucking Beckett's fingers like they were his cock. *Are they going to expect me to fuck them again? It was hot, but—*

"Don't worry, Princess. We won't fuck you. We won't even touch you, not now that you're *forbidden*," Hayes says with a chuckle.

Lennox and Caius join him in laughter.

"I wouldn't laugh if I were you guys. Everyone here is in danger. Vincent has a video of you all fucking me, and he's not happy. If he finds out it was you guys, you're all dead."

"We knew the risk we took that night, and we would all do it again. You wanted control over your life; we helped you get it," Caius says, stretching as he takes a seat on the couch.

I look over to Beckett.

"Don't worry about me. I haven't slept with you. I'm perfectly safe from Corsi's wrath," Beckett answers with a smirk without looking up from the laptop, like he knows it bothers me that we haven't fucked and never will.

Suddenly, Beckett's eyes widen. "Gage, Caius, come here."

They both run behind the couch so they can stare at the same screen. Hayes heads back to the kitchen, and Lennox opens his own laptop on the couch. I'm left standing in the entryway, unsure what I'm supposed to do. *Join them in the living room? Head to one of the bedrooms?*

"Look where he is. He went straight to Corsi's. Do you think Corsi had Nolan do it to keep his hands clean?" Beckett asks.

Caius's face darkens. "He looked bored and disinterested like he knew he had this game in the bag and Corsi would put him through. Now we know why. There is definitely a connection there. We need to find out what."

"I'll start digging," Lennox says.

Gage leans in. "Me too. We'll know exactly who this guy is and what he does by tomorrow."

Caius runs his hand through his hair, and then he heads upstairs without a word—an emotionless zombie just going through life.

The guys watch him walk off without speaking; everyone has concern in their eyes except for Lennox.

"I should go check on him," Hayes says.

"No, you shouldn't. He needs time. He just lost his sister. Don't push him. I'll let you know when you should push him," Lennox says.

The room goes silent, and Lennox meets my gaze. I see it finally. The pain. The loss. He's lost someone.

He cocks his head to the side as he studies me. His eyes narrow, and his lips part, trying to read my mind. I know he sees my own pain, my own loss, but he doesn't say anything. He just goes back to his laptop.

But I see my opening, my chance to help and show Beckett I'm on his side, and he should be on mine.

"I can get information about Nolan for you. You can take me back to Vincent's condo later under the guise that I'm getting some of my belongings for the week. I can poke around, ask the security guards, get into Vincent's office." I could even ask Vincent himself. He'd tell me, but it would mean I would owe him something. I don't tell Beckett that, though. It's hard to keep track of everyone I owe a debt to —Vincent, Caius, and Beckett.

No one moves as I speak. The only thing I notice is Beckett's nostrils slowly widening then narrowing with each breath. I'm not even sure he's blinked.

Then he slides the computer off his lap, stands, and walks slowly toward me.

I don't move. I hold my ground.

If he wants to hurt me to put me in my place, I'll fight back. I know how—I proved that tonight. He may have won in that box, but I'll at least get a good punch or kick to the balls in.

He seems to notice the twinkle in my eyes and the sway of my hips as I get balanced, ready to throw a punch or kick or dodge one.

"Tell me why I should believe you're anything but daddy's dirty little whore?"

I frown.

"That you're not just pretty arm candy that your father parades around as a reward when really all you are is a gold digger, happy to play the part so someday she can play with her new husband's credit card."

My ears burn red. "I—"

He cuts me off. "Tell me why I should trust you when you're nothing but a sleazy seductress whose game it is to make men fall at her knees or fight each other to the death for her? That's what we're doing, isn't it? I may have come up with the game, but your father and you turned it into a deathmatch. Only one man is going to survive—the man your father deems worthy. You don't care who that is as long as he's filthy rich."

I flinch at every hurtful word he spits my way. He's angry—at me, my father, the world. I thought his grief would start slowly getting better. Very slowly, like fog in the morning getting thinner until one day it's just gone, nothing but a memory. But he's only become even more broken and cynical. I'm afraid his grief is going to keep boring into him until it consumes him.

"You know why we call you Princess? Because that's what you are. A slutty princess who does other people's bidding."

My hand moves to slap him as his words sting my own cheek. Every word is hurtful and cruel. Every word is laced with his heartbreak. He may need to get the words out, but it doesn't mean I have to stand here and take it.

He pulls his head back, and I miss. His movement is automatic; he didn't have to think about it at all.

"Tell me, Princess, why should I trust you when all you've ever done is cause me pain? You don't care about me. You don't care about any of us. All these guys behind me feel the exact same way. All you care about is you. So stop trying to prove your loyalty to me; it's not going to end well."

And then he turns and storms away. I hear the echo of a glass door shutting on his way out of the cabin.

I'm left speechless.

Lennox stands, glaring at me as he heads to his room. Even Hayes, who usually is carefree and will talk to me about anything, is speechless as he walks to his room.

"Odette's funeral is tomorrow. That's why Beckett and Caius are acting the way they are. It's not personal," Gage says, picking up his laptop.

"Isn't it?"

Gage shrugs.

"Sleep on the couch and don't make trouble, not tonight. If you try to run, if you try anything, Beckett will kill you. And then Corsi will kill him. So if you care about him at all, then sleep and stay in the house all day tomorrow. That's how you gain a sliver of his trust."

Then Gage leaves me alone in the living room.

Odette's funeral is tomorrow.

They haven't even buried her yet.

Of course, his grief is escalating. Of course, he blames me.

I lie down on the couch, not even bothering to change into anything more comfortable or wrap myself in a blanket. It won't matter anyway.

My sleep tonight is going to be restless, filled with terrors and nightmares of my own grief returning. Just like the fog in the mountains, it always comes back, until it slowly slips away once more. But tonight, my grief will hang around like a heavy fog; I won't be able to escape it.

10

BECKETT

I straighten my black tie as I look in the mirror. I hate ties. It's one of those skills that took me forever to learn after my accident. It's hard enough with two good hands, but with only one hand now, it's a challenge.

I considered using my prosthetic arm packed away in one of my bags, but even the thought of having to tie a tie couldn't make me put that thing on. Some people like using prosthetics, but I don't deserve to replace what I lost. And at Odette's funeral, I want to be myself. Just myself, nothing more.

I could have asked one of the guys for help, but I didn't. I wanted to be by myself before we leave. As soon as I step foot outside this bedroom door, I'm going to be surrounded by people, when all I want is to be alone with my thoughts.

No, all I want is Odette back.

It's the one thing I can never have.

There's a soft knock on the door, and Hayes says, "Five minutes."

He doesn't wait for an answer before I hear his feet descend the stairs. He must have drawn the short straw.

I adjust the tie one more time, ensuring it's perfect before walking out of the bedroom. For once, I don't mind wearing a suit—anything to honor Odette.

I head downstairs, expecting to see everyone waiting for me. However, the room is empty and quiet except for Ri's soft moans as she sleeps on the couch. No, tosses and turns in a fit is more like it. Her lips tremble as she speaks in her sleep to whatever monster she sees in her mind. Sweat mats her hair down her face, but her body trembles as if she's freezing.

"No, please, no. It can't be true..." she says.

I freeze, intent on listening to whatever torments her so I can use it against her later. Instead, she just turns over, away from me. She doesn't murmur any other words.

Caius comes down the stairs. He looks at me, then her, with a coldness in his eyes.

I hope he's able to grieve today, feel something. Scream, yell, cry, punch someone—anything that shows he's still in there. Before her death, Caius and I used to be good friends. Now, all that's left of him is an empty shell.

He watches her tremble. He sees the throw blanket at her feet. He does nothing to comfort her. He doesn't cover her. He doesn't wake her from her nightmares. He doesn't hold her. He does none of the things the old Caius would have done. He just looks at me one more time, then walks out.

I stare down at Ri, hoping she'll give me any clue as to what she's dreaming about. She doesn't speak.

My heart hardens watching her.

She took what was mine. She took Odette from me.

I know it's ridiculous to place all the blame on her. If

she played a part in her death, it was a small one. Ri was with me when Odette was taken and eventually killed. But Ri is the only target I have.

I reach down, my hand feeling the pulse in her delicate neck. It's thundering.

I may have called her a whore, weak, pathetic, a gold digger. That may all be true, but there is one thing she is above all that—fierce.

I stroke her neck, resisting my desire to strangle her in her sleep. I'm about to walk away, when I spot the throw blanket at her feet again. I may be heartless, but she's mine. And I need her alive long enough to torture later.

So I cover her with the blanket, and her trembles ease. But that's all I'll do to help her. I'm heartless now.

Then I walk out to find the others loaded up in one of the SUVs. I climb into the passenger seat. Lennox is driving, and the other three are in the back.

"You good?" Lennox asks. I know it's the only time he'll ask, although I doubt it will be the last time I hear that or a similar question.

I nod, but I'll never be good again.

We arrive at a small country-looking church. The exterior white walls could use some new paint in a few places, but its dark steeple still holds strong against the luscious green surroundings. You wouldn't know we're only a couple of hours from the city. You'd think we are in the middle of unending farmland.

I wasn't involved much in the planning. Mr. Monroe said he'd take care of the details, that I had more important things to worry about in getting retribution for her.

Part of me wishes I would have been more involved, though. Odette wasn't really religious. I don't recall her enjoying farmland or the countryside. The only thing I can say about this place is it's private and peaceful. At least that part Odette would have appreciated.

And she would have been at home with the hoard of people filing into the church. I, on the other hand, want to run from all of these people. There are a few faces I recognize as I stand in the grass just outside the car, staring at people as they slowly enter. Family members she introduced me to or friends of hers, but most of the faces are unfamiliar.

Caius gets out of the car and walks straight to his father, with Lennox following behind. I guess Lennox has assigned himself to Caius today in case he explodes. I don't know Lennox's full story, but I do know from hushed conversations that he's lost someone. He's the only one truly experienced with this kind of grief.

That leaves Hayes and Gage to babysit me. Hayes stands awkwardly to my left with his hands in his pockets. He opens and closes his mouth several times but says nothing. Gage isn't as tepid.

"Most everyone here belongs to the Retribution Kings. They are all on your side. They want you to be the leader. They want you to succeed with initiation. You don't need to see any of them as a threat. If you want to be introduced to anyone, you can. If you want to be left alone, you can. It's up to you," Gage says.

But I know it's bullshit. It may be my wife's funeral, but this is the first time they've seen me after I found out why I was chosen. After I found out that Odette was the daughter of the leader of the Retribution Kings. That Mr. Monroe is dying. That I am expected to take his place.

I can't look weak, not even here. If I want the role that Odette married me for, then I have to be strong. I have to look them all in the eye. I have to grieve without tears, without wearing my heart on my sleeve, without emotion outside of wanting revenge. I have to be the boss they want me to be, or I'll lose everything I have left.

And I need to take care of retribution for Odette myself.

I start walking toward the church, my shoulders back, my head held high, no tears or overly grief-stricken look in my eyes. I let the need to punish those responsible overwhelm anything else I feel.

Everyone stares, stopping everything else they are doing as they watch me walk with Gage and Hayes behind me. I don't stop for introductions. It doesn't matter to me who any of them are, just that they know who I am.

Several men nod at me as I walk, as if they already accept me. Others tense like they already fear me. A few hold tears in their eyes. I ignore them all as I walk into the church.

A woman at the entrance hands me a program. She gives me a tired smile. "I'm sorry for your loss," the gray-haired woman says.

My jaw tenses. I hate those words, although they're the first time they've been spoken to me. I nod solemnly and continue down the aisle of the church. Each step I take, I can hear the gentle creak of the wooden floor. I focus on that and not the unending faces of sorrow staring back at me.

Mr. Monroe and Caius are already sitting in the first pew, with Lennox sitting in the second row. Lennox notices me first and gives me a brief nod of reassurance before he stands to let Gage and Hayes in.

"Mr. Monroe—" I start, but then I realize I don't know how to finish that sentence, certainly not with 'I'm sorry for your loss' or 'How are you holding up,' so my words drop.

He moves to stand, reaching for his cane.

"No, don't get up."

He growls, almost like I insulted him. He grabs his cane, and this time I don't interject. I don't even offer a hand to help him.

His knees creak, his back hunches forward, and his hand shakes on the cane before he finally gets enough momentum to stand. When his eyes meet mine, I see nothing but the proud man, the leader, the boss, the king of all those who chose to join him in his mission—a mission I still don't fully understand.

He holds out his left hand to me.

I stare at it a moment before I take it with my own left hand. It's an awkward moment.

"Today, we mourn the loss of Odette, but it's also the start of a new day. I may have lost a daughter, but I gained a son. Soon, I'll be buried right next to her. Prove that we chose correctly," he says.

I've never wanted to hit an old, dying man before, but I do now.

We chose.

WE.

This was all a business arrangement. I never got to ask Odette if any part of it was real for her before she was killed. That's what Mr. Monroe is reminding me. The emotion I show should reflect that.

Somehow I gather enough strength to nod and walk to my seat beside Caius without using his cane to whack him over the head with it. How dare he remind me at my wife's funeral that it was never about love. That it was all a lie. That my grief isn't as important as his or Caius's. That my grief shouldn't impact my ability to show that I'm a true leader.

They *chose* correctly...

I want to destroy them all. If it wasn't for them, Odette would still be alive. She wouldn't have been pressured to date me. Maybe she wouldn't have even met me.

The minister starts, but I barely pay attention. None of the words he speaks are real. None of this is real. My marriage wasn't even real.

I stare down at the program and see Odette's smiling face back at me. *It wasn't real.*

I twist the program in my lap.

I want to run out and punch anyone who stands in my way.

I want to scream.

Cry.

Lose myself in a bottle of whiskey.

Forget everything else.

Even my need for revenge.

Revenge for Odette.

Revenge for me.

But then I see it—her casket.

It's being carried by six men into the church.

It's white with gold trim and light pink flowers on top.

I sit up straighter, straining to look closer, trying to understand why there's a casket. *Is it just because it feels wrong to hold a service without a casket?*

Gage leans forward until he can whisper to me. "Corsi arranged for Mayhem to return her body."

———

I stare at the pile of dirt covered in flowers over where I just watched Odette's casket be buried. Most people have begun to leave, but a few still hang around.

"I need to help my dad home," Caius says.

I nod. It's the only reaction I know how to give that won't break me.

Caius leads his father away, with Lennox trailing him. Neither of them broke. No tears were shed. No emotion shown. They only displayed strength. I don't know how they did it. *How did they endure listening to endless words spoken about someone who was a daughter, a sister?*

"Go with them," I say to Gage and Hayes. But it's not just them I say it to. My friends, my oldest family—Enzo, Kai, Zeke, Siren, Langston, and Liesel stand beyond the trees, watching but not getting close enough that anyone but me knows they are here. As much as they'd ease my grief, I can't go to them. I can't talk to them. I have to show my loyalty to the Retribution Kings, even if I want to slaughter them all for their part in Odette's death. Seeing my friends would just remind me of more pain from my past that I'm not ready to face—not today.

"You sure, man? We—" Hayes says.

"Yes, I need to be alone," I say as clearly as I can, knowing they'll be reading my lips.

"I'll make sure we leave the keys in the car for you."

I nod, watching as my friends nod too.

And then I turn back to her grave.

"You loved her, didn't you?" a voice says next to me, startling me.

I look at the unknown man out of the corner of my eye. He's an older man, maybe early sixties. I assume he's part of the Retribution Kings, whatever that means, so I don't know how I should answer. Stoically, like I'm not bothered that she's dead, or...

"Yes, I loved her," I answer, honestly.

"I can tell. I lost my wife five years ago."

"I'm sorry."

He waves me off. "Nothing to be sorry about. You didn't kill her; that bastard cancer did."

I put my hand in my pocket and nod.

"Odette was far too young to die."

"She was."

"You blame yourself, don't you?"

I nod.

"It's Beckett, right?"

I nod.

"I'm Walter. Beckett, let me tell you something. Monroe, he..." He shakes his head. "He knew the risks. He knew he should have protected his daughter better. He should have told you the truth sooner. Instead, he let you two live the fairytale for far too long without ensuring the dragon was slain first. This isn't your fault, son. It's his and our enemies."

I stare at the mountain of flowers that will soon decay into the earth, just like Odette. His words don't make the pain in my chest any softer.

"It was the mafia, wasn't it? They killed her."

I nod, sure deep in my bones that it was Corsi. Why, I'm still not sure, but I will.

"The mafia, you know what they're good for?"

I shake my head.

"Revenge."

I stare at him.

"But we're better. They seek revenge by simply killing. We get revenge by taking everything from them, destroying everyone they love, and only then do we offer mercy by killing them," he finishes. He pats me on my shoulder, and then he walks away. He's the last to leave. And then it's just me and Odette.

I fall to my knees, wishing the skies would open up. I wish rain, lightning, thunder would descend on me and hide my emotions. But of course, mother nature doesn't respond.

I slam my fist into the pile of dirt.

"How could you?

"How could you lie to me?

"How could you make me fall in love with you?"

Each comes out louder than the previous, until...

"How could you...how could you leave me?" explodes from my chest as tears flow and flow. Anger and heart-break swirl becoming one until I won't be able to separate them.

I feel something wet on my forehead.

I look up.

Rain.

I stayed so long that I finally got my wish.

Only after the rain has washed away any remnants of my grief do I finally get up, walk alone back to the car, and drive it back to the cabin.

My mind is blank as I walk up the gravel drive toward the front door, the rain still falling heavily from the sky. I welcome every drop on my face.

I stumble to a stop when I see her standing in the grass in the backyard; her hands spread wide as the rain pelts her face.

I narrow my eyes as I stare and find myself walking toward her. I tell myself it's just to see what crazy thing she's doing now—probably trying to signal to her father as one of his guys waits in the lake.

But as I near her, I realize she's doing the same thing I was at Odette's grave—mourning.

Slowly, she turns, and I see her face. She studies mine as I study hers.

I realize something—not even the rain can hide her grief. Which means it can't hide mine.

I can still see her puffy, red eyes. Her swollen face. Her exhausted lips. Weak and tired body. She can't hide any of it.

Her eyes roam over my body, and I know she sees the same on me.

I don't know what or who she's grieving.

She a narcissistic princess who only cares about herself.

She doesn't get to choose her husband.

Guilt for causing the death of an innocent woman.

Or loss for someone she cared about?

None of it matters.

What matters is I need the pain to stop in order to complete my mission, to carry out retribution.

I look her dead in the eye and say, "Want to earn my hero services, Princess?"

11

BECKETT

Ri's anger flares at my words.

I know the feeling, Sweetheart. Everything she says stirs dark thoughts in my mind.

"You want me to trust you? Here's your chance. You do something for me; I'll play hero for you the next time you need it. Although, based on your last performance, it seems you can easily save yourself, Princess."

No matter what you do, Princess, I still won't trust you. I can see the agony of loss all over your face, the secrets you're hiding.

Her lips move like she wants to speak, and then she tucks her lips in, frowning.

"Say it, whatever's on your mind. It's not like we are standing out here in the pouring rain or anything."

She folds her arms as her anger intensifies. "No one said you had to join me. And you really don't want to hear what I have to say."

"I don't, but if you don't say it, you'll stew and use it against me later."

"I just—I just wanted you to know I understand how hard today was for you. I wish I could say it gets easier from here. It doesn't. Grief is a strange thing—some moments you think you've moved past it and then a song, a smell, a road you drive down, anything will spark a memory, and it can overpower you once again.

"And then, one time out of a hundred, you finally get that memory that doesn't spark unbearable grief. It could be the smallest thing, an inside joke you shared or how your toes curl when you kiss her, or how it felt to have your arms wrapped around her, and that memory is going to make you feel alive like you haven't in days, weeks, months. It will remind you that having her, however brief, was worth all the heart-wrecking pain. It will still hurt that she's gone, but you'll remember why you have to keep living—keep chasing those little moments."

She looks down, water dripping from her lashes. She's still wearing the same clothes from before—a sparkly tank and black pants, but she's barefoot now. Her clothes are stuck to her body from standing in the rain for so long; I'm sure I could see her nipples poking through her shirt if it wasn't for the rain.

She's vulnerable in this moment, sharing a part of her truth, that she's been through this too. And while I appreciate it, all I want to do is take advantage of her vulnerability. I can't face my own.

"Do we have a deal or not?" I ask, ignoring the fact that she just poured her heart out to me.

She runs her hand through her hair, flipping it back like that's going to keep the rain from her face.

"Deal." She licks her lips, more than ready ever for a fight. That's what this deal we have is—a fight, a power struggle, our own miniature battle to see who is better at manipulating whom.

She's definitely trying to manipulate me as much as I am her. I need to learn why. It has to be because of the Retribution Kings, which means I need to learn more about who they are and what they do. What they protect. What their secrets are. What she could want to learn.

I hear gravel crunching behind us; the guys are back. I don't know if she notices; the rain is still coming down hard enough that she might not yet.

I want to embarrass her.

I want the thrill of hurting her and seeing her desperation to do whatever I want. I wasn't this way with Odette. I wasn't a controlling monster, but Ri brings out the worst of me.

"Take off your shirt."

"Wh—"

"Did I ask you to talk back? If you want me to play hero for you, then you do this without question."

"I thought you liked my talking back."

My nostrils flare. *She's right; I do like it.* "Talk back and see how much worse this gets for you."

The SUV doors slam shut, and I know she heard them. I don't know if they'll walk back here to find us or head into the house.

"Do your worst, Hero." And then she removes her shirt in one fluid movement, like she's done this a hundred times in front of me.

Fuck me.

No, there will be no fucking. I just lost my wife.

Your lying wife, who didn't even care about you. She was just doing what her father told her.

Even the rain can't hide how beautiful her naked chest is. Soft mounds rise on her chest with each heavy breath. Scars that some might see as ugly, I see as proof of her strength. She's fought and won time and time again. I want more. I want to see everything.

"I know why you hate me," she says.

"Because you took everything from me and don't know how to keep your mouth shut?" I say.

"No, because I remind you of Odette."

I laugh at that. "You are nothing like Odette. She was sweet, good-natured, wouldn't hurt a fly. You're savage, malicious, and violent."

She shakes her head. "I didn't mean personality-wise. You think I'm controlled by my father just like she was."

I frown. She's right, but I won't admit that.

She puts her hands on her hips, pushing her breasts out as rain drips down over her peaked nipples. Her eyes flit past me to, I'm sure, one of the guys, then back to me.

"The other reason—you want me, just like you wanted her."

I chuckle deviously. "I want to fuck you, just like every man behind me wants to fuck you again. But the difference between them and me? I want to destroy you more."

"You can't destroy what's already demolished."

"You are far from destroyed, Princess. From what I can see, you're a wall of strength that I'll enjoy cracking slowly until you crumble and fall."

She shivers from the rain, from my words.

"Take off your pants."

I expect her to look at the other guys. To blush like a dainty princess who hasn't already been naked in front of all of us before, hasn't fucked everyone but me. But I guess we're done playing games and pretending.

Her pants and panties fall to her feet before I can blink; then, she's standing naked in front of me.

I take my time surveying her body. My eyes roam over every curve, every imperfection, every piece of skin I crave to kiss, touch, taste. Skin that is mine, and yet I won't allow myself to touch.

I don't know how much time passes. A stroke of lightning and thunder brings me back to reality.

Ri shakes uncontrollably even as she tries to remain strong. Rain drips off my suit jacket in spades.

"Kneel," I finally say, my voice deeper than the thunder.

She falls to her knees as if she's been dying to do just that this entire time.

"Spread your legs."

She bites her plump bottom lip, but her smile shines through. "Don't forget that I'm forbidden, Hero. You fuck me and it will be your funeral next."

I growl, letting her know that she got under my skin.

"Make yourself come, Princess. Make your mouth useful for once and tell me everything you're doing, everything you're thinking while you're doing it."

She chuckles. "I don't know how this is punishment, but okay."

Oh, it's punishment, alright—punishment for me.

I look behind me and find all four of the bastards. Hayes and Gage are leaning against the siding, eyes glued to her body and probably reliving the night they got to fuck her. They better keep that memory because it will be the only time. I won't let them risk their lives to fuck her again.

Yea, keep telling yourself that. It has nothing to do with thinking you own her ass.

Caius is standing to my left with his hands in his pockets. He looks like death, like he hasn't slept in a year. He still doesn't show any emotion.

Even Lennox is watching, albeit, from further away than the rest. But he still doesn't go into the house.

They must know if I didn't want them here, I would order them to go into the house. They're right. I want them here to ensure I don't go too far.

We aren't close as a group. I never asked to be their leader. I haven't even earned their loyalty. But they are all I have left of Odette. And maybe one day, I'll earn their loyalty.

"I'm waiting," I bark.

She smirks. "Still don't see how this is punishment." Slowly, one of her hands slides over her chest until she holds one of her swollen breasts in her hand. She lets her thumb brush over her nipple, while her other hand pauses on her stomach, near the beautiful space between her legs.

"Why so quiet? I know you like to talk."

She licks her lips, rain mixing with her saliva.

"What are you thinking, Ri?" I ask.

"I'm thinking about how much you want me. How you want to lose control, pick me up, grab my ass. I wrap my legs around your waist as you carry me through the house to your bedroom. You'll slip into me before we make it, though, and I'll let out a cry so loud that all these assholes will eavesdrop, wishing I was fucking them instead of you."

I glare at her as my cock comes to life in my pants. *Damn her.*

"That sounds an awful lot like I'm your hero in this scenario."

"Maybe I don't need to be saved from some monster. Maybe I just want you to whisk me away and play the hero when you fuck me. So that for once, I don't have to be the strong one."

"Not going to happen, Princess. I save you from others, not yourself, and definitely not me."

She sighs.

"While I love the direct view of your pussy, I doubt you can make yourself come from just touching your breasts."

"Oh, I'm very talented. I could make myself come with just my dirty thoughts."

"Fine, then do it, and I'll owe you—*anything*. I'll play hero however you want."

Her eyes light up.

She wants to fuck me, fix me, prove to me that I can be with a woman again after Odette.

But I have a theory, and I'm willing to bet everything on it.

"Make yourself come, Ri, without touching that swollen pink clit of yours," my voice is heady, full of need and want. It should help her, but I think it's going to do the opposite.

She runs her tongue over her teeth as she pinches her nipple, rubbing her other hand over her soaking thighs.

"You're going to regret this," she says, her voice deep and sultry.

I eye her carefully. Either way, I win. Either way, I lose.

I put my hand in the pocket of my jacket. It's soaked. I'm soaked. I should go inside instead of playing these games, but this is worth getting pneumonia.

She starts to close her eyes, but we can't have that.

"Look at me, Princess. I need proof when you come."

"Then you need to be looking at my pussy, not my

eyes. Or better yet, slide a finger inside if you really want to check." She winks at me as her breathing gets heavier.

"No, your eyes. Your eyes can't lie to me."

Her eyes roam up and down my body. She stimulates her nipples more; the rain continues to pelt us. Her body trembles slightly while her moans leave her lips. I watch as the rain hits between her legs, hitting her clit and probably pushing her toward the edge. *Maybe this was a mistake I'm destined to lose.*

Her moans get louder, telling me she's close. I underestimated her. My theory was wrong.

I hold her gaze, waiting for the moment she explodes.

It never comes.

She never comes.

"You okay there, Princess? If that was an orgasm, it was pathetic. Nothing like what I'm sure these guys induced from you."

She snarls at me.

I squat down, so we are eye to eye. And okay, yes, so I can get a better view of her. I'm really regretting asking for that rain at this point, even if it is hot as hell to see her dripping with water.

"I'll give you one more chance. Touch yourself between your legs. Rub that little bundle of nerves you're aching to press. Make yourself come, and I'll keep our new agreement. I'll do anything you want."

"If you want to fuck me so badly, just say it," she snarks back.

"That's a lot of talk for someone who still hasn't proven she can make herself come."

Her fingers dive between her folds, slamming against her swollen clit. She thinks she's going to end this quickly.

I still don't think she's going to win.

I stand back up, watching her carefully. My cock is painfully hard in my pants.

I watch her a few minutes, rubbing in circles, stroking, sliding fingers up inside her wet pussy. But she's no closer to coming than she was when she was just rubbing her breasts and thinking dirty thoughts.

I can see the frustration on her face. She's a fierce one. She has no problem being naked and touching herself in front of me or any of the others, but she still can't come.

I decide to push her further while also relieving myself of some of the pain. It will still be plenty of punishment.

I undo my pants and pull my cock out.

Her eyes go wide as she stops what she's doing and watches me stroke my hard length.

"You're not going to make yourself come if you stop."

"What...what are you doing?"

I'm pretty sure she's drooling, but it's hard to tell in the rain.

"Racing you. Pretty sure I can make myself come a dozen times before you even succeed once."

The spark flickers in her eyes. She likes a good competition, but it still won't be enough. She won't make herself come. She won't win.

She pinches her clit before rubbing her fingers over it in fast, punishing circles.

I stroke my cock in hard, pushing strokes matching her own fury.

Our eyes glue together in a battle.

I could come in two seconds flat. I've been aching far too long, but I force myself to hold back and have more time to watch her.

I can see the defeat in her eyes. She pushes harder once more, but then her fingers slow. Her shoulders slump. Her eyes drift from mine to Caius.

I keep stroking, but then I see the concern flicker in her eyes at the sight of Caius. It's the same one I felt.

She doesn't show that concern when she looks at me. She doesn't soften with me; she hardens. She fights.

And then I do something I never thought I would. I walk forward.

"Open," I say, grabbing her hair as I shove my cock between her lips before either of us can think about it.

I break my vow not to touch her, not to feel good with her. It shatters me. I won't last, but then that's not the point. I've crossed a line, and now that it's crossed, there is no going back. I'm going to want more. I'll try to deny myself, punish myself, but I won't be able to. I've gotten a taste of the forbidden apple, and I want more.

She gasps at first, but then she wraps her lips around my cock like a pro. I don't give her time to adjust or even catch her breath. I pump deep into her mouth until I'm hitting the back of her throat. My grip on her hair tightens into a fist as I tilt her head up to look at me.

The rain drives down harder, picking up as I drive my cock into her faster. Rain hits her eyes, her nose, her cheeks. She gags and struggles against my cock. Still, just a whisper of my fingers against the lips between her legs, and she'd explode too.

Too bad I'm a cruel man.

Too bad I'm more intent on winning than letting her get a release.

I can't hold back my own release. I come hard down her throat, only pulling out after she's taken my full load.

Her throat bobbing up and down as my cum pours down her throat.

I tuck myself back into my pants before I lean down and whisper so only she can hear me.

"You know why you couldn't come?"

She shakes her head.

"Because I told you to. You hate taking orders. You refuse to take them, which means one of two things. You do what Corsi says because he has someone you love, or you do it because you want to. That way it isn't really an order. I think it's the second one. Either way, it doesn't matter to me. Either way, you are no use to me."

Her lips fall apart, her big eyes shine, and then she shakes so hard that I'm afraid she did just catch pneumonia.

"Leave," I order, loudly.

She moves to get up.

"Not you."

"Oh," she whispers.

I don't take my eyes off her, but I wait until I no longer hear the crunch of gravel, and I hear the door slam shut.

Then, I scoop her up in my arm.

"What are you doing?"

"Quiet. Don't say a word, or I'll remember why I shouldn't do this."

She quirks an eyebrow but is silent as I carry her into the house.

The guys have smartly made themselves scarce as I carry her against my chest. My one arm is doing most of the work, but just like her naughty fairytale, she wraps her legs around my waist and loops her arms around my neck. My hand finds her bare ass.

She's still naked.

I'm still soaked in my suit.

I carry her up the stairs to my bedroom.

I drop her onto the bed.

She reaches for a blanket.

"Don't."

She pauses, still trembling. I know she's cold. I know she needs to warm up. But she's not doing it with a damn blanket.

"I'm breaking all the rules." I think about Corsi's rule. She's forbidden. *Fuck her and you lose. Fuck her and you die.*

I guess it depends on what his definition of fucking her is.

I grin as I forget who I am. I forget about my past, about my future, about how I hate this girl lying on my bed.

I kneel over her on the bed. "Spread your legs."

They fall apart, as do her lips. Her heart rate is probably through the roof, as is mine.

Don't think, just do.

I press my lips against her clit, tasting the sweet mixture of her and the rain. She tastes like the earth, like a goddess more than a princess. Sweeter than she should be, a tiny bit heavenly.

I don't know what this is.

Revenge at Odette for lying.

Proof that I can make Ri come when she can't.

Manipulation of her heart to fall for me before I destroy her.

Or maybe this taste is just for me. Just because I fucking want to.

Whatever the reason, I don't regret tasting her. I don't regret two seconds later when she's falling apart. Her moans reach every room in this house. She doesn't say my name, but she will next time.

Next time...

There's going to be a fucking next time, a time where I fuck her exactly how I want, consequences be dammed. She can have my cock, I own her, but she'll never get my heart.

12

RI

I'M SPEECHLESS.

It's not something I'm used to feeling. I usually have a snarky comment for everything, but not this. This I have no words for. All I have are overwhelming feelings.

God, that was—fucking magical. The intense connection, the spark, how Beckett makes me feel when he touches me. Jesus, if I could bottle that feeling and drink it whenever I needed it, I wouldn't need food or water or air to survive, just this feeling.

The feeling doesn't vanish when Beckett does either. It's too strong, too all-consuming, too much.

I need more.

I'm naked, lying on top of Beckett's bed, soaking wet from the rain and from the powerful orgasm Beckett just pried from me.

The shivers start again. I need to dry off, shower, and climb into a warm bed so I don't get sick. But if I shower, it will wash away Beckett's scent, and I'm afraid he's already come to his senses. He won't be returning to this bed, not as long as I'm in it.

He's already regretting what he did. Not because I'm forbidden, but because he feels ashamed. His wife is gone. His wife betrayed him. Her love for him might not even have been real. She had a job to do, and she did it. But it doesn't stop him from loving her.

And if he still loves her, he hates himself for touching me.

He didn't fuck me—but I know this was my one night. This was my one chance to feel his lips, his tongue, his fingers against me. To feel him lose himself in me. To remind him that his life does go on.

That was all I'll get, though.

We may still play our games. He may still have me do degrading things in order for him to save me. He may even win the stupid game and marry me, but he won't touch me or fuck me—never again.

So even as goosebumps race over my arms, every hair on my body raises, and my body shakes uncontrollably from the cold, I don't move. I just relish the feeling.

Beckett's the one.

My other half.

I can't explain why I know. Why, deep in my gut, I know, but I do. I just see the world a little differently when he's around. I'm ready to fight, ready to take on the world when he's near.

But he'll never be mine.

I squeeze my eyes shut to keep my pain locked away.

He'll never be mine.

That is the thought that finally gets me out of bed and into the shower, where I do my best to wash Beckett away.

Wash away his deranged orders that terrified me and also turned me on.

Wash away that I couldn't come without his touch.

Wash away that I want him. I could love him if he let me, if the world let me.

I can't.

My life isn't my own.

I can't have him.

That's the thought that I hold onto as I finally drift to sleep while staring at the door, waiting for it to open, knowing it won't, but hoping it would anyway.

———

The smell of coffee wakes me up. I look over at the other side of the bed, but I know that Beckett isn't there. He never came back.

I do my business in the connecting bathroom and assume I'm going to have to find some of Beckett's clothes to put on. But then I spot a pile on the bathroom counter: leggings, sports bra, tank, and running shoes.

I put them on, pulling my ratted hair into a messy bun on top of my head and wiping the remnants of my mascara off from under my eyes. Then I head downstairs toward the heavenly smell of caffeine.

No one is in the kitchen, so I help myself to a cup of coffee. I'm leaning against the small cabin counter and considering my next move when I hear a loud grunt and then guys chuckling.

I walk to the glass door at the back and see Hayes on his ass as Gage triumphantly grins down at him. Caius, Lennox, and Beckett are sitting in camping chairs, chuckling as Hayes wipes blood from his forehead.

I take a deep breath, considering staying inside and just watching from here. But I can't hide forever. I need to face them, all of them.

So I throw the door open and step out into the sun, holding my cup of coffee like a weapon I plan on using on all of them.

All five pairs of eyes shoot toward me. Hayes's and Gage's smile at me. Lennox's eyes roll. Caius's eyes hold but don't allow me any deeper. And Beckett's fill with desire, or maybe that's just my imagination.

I ignore him and look down at Hayes, who is still sitting on his ass on the ground, no doubt put there by Gage, who is still standing over him. Both of the guys look hot as hell. Hayes has removed his glasses, and his hair is in a low messy bun. Gage is wearing a tight shirt that shows off his muscles as sweat drizzles down his forehead.

"What'd you say to get your ass beaten so early?" I ask Hayes.

"Nothing. You know I don't have a smart mouth. I leave that to you, Princess," Hayes says with a sexy grin.

I shake my head at him and grip my coffee with two hands as I take another sip.

Gage reaches his hand out to Hayes, who takes it and is helped to his feet.

"We were just training," Gage says.

"Looks like Hayes could use some more training," I tease.

"Ouch, way to hit a man when he's already down," Hayes feigns being shot in the chest, but then his eyes fill with lust.

I look from guy to guy, and that's all I see—lust.

They're remembering me naked on my knees, touching myself.

"Cute—she gets embarrassed the next morning, but not when she's naked and touching herself," Lennox says.

I glare at him.

Gage steps between me and Lennox. "Woah, cool off, Princess. You don't want to get into a fight with Knox."

"Maybe I do," I puff my chest out.

Lennox snickers. "Let's go." But he doesn't move from his chair.

"Maybe we should let her fight him," Beckett says.

All heads turn to him.

"What? Why would we do that? She'd get her ass kicked," Hayes says.

I frown, hating his comment.

"We can't let her fight; we have to keep her safe. If she comes back bloodied and beaten, Corsi will eliminate us from the game," Caius says.

"That's sweet, Charming, but Len would actually have to hit me for that to happen. And only Vincent said you couldn't fuck me and you had to return me safe. Even if he did manage to hit me, I'd have a week to recover, and it's nothing a little makeup wouldn't cover up anyway," I say.

Caius looks concerned, as does Gage.

Hayes lights up like he wants to see this.

Lennox raises an eyebrow, ready to go if I am.

Everyone turns to Beckett. He'll have the last word. He'll decide whether I fight or not.

"We need to know how good she is, for real. Is she willing to give it all she's got and not hold back? You willing to do that, Princess?" Beckett goads me. He knows it will work. I can't turn down a challenge.

I down the rest of my coffee and then set the mug down on a deck step behind me. Then I stretch my arms and neck. "Ready when you are, Len."

"No," Beckett says, just as Lennox is about to stand up.

"Afraid I'm going to kick his ass? Need to lay some ground rules first, Hero?"

"Lennox is the best fighter among us; you earn the right to fight him. Start with Hayes."

"Hey, I'm not that bad," Hayes says.

Everyone chuckles.

Hayes sighs. "Fine, I'll fight her. What are the rules?"

Beckett studies me, but then he looks back to Hayes. "What are you best at?"

"I was a wrestler in high school."

"Wrestling rules then. The first to takedown the other wins. Play as dirty as you want, though," Beckett grins, and I swear he winks at me.

He thinks I'll win.

I know I'll win.

Beckett looks to me. "You want to gain my trust? Show me what you got. Show me you're as good as you think you are."

I roll my eyes as I stretch my arms behind my back. I'd rather have some time to jog and warm up my muscles properly before I fight, but this will have to do.

"Ready to do this, Heartbreaker?"

Hayes laughs. "I'm ready to get you under me again, Princess. You aren't forbidden to me, just them."

I laugh. "Oh, you're forbidden from touching me without my permission."

"Too bad I'm stronger than you." He grabs me before I have a chance to move, tucking me against his body. His arm goes in front of my chest as my ass presses against his front. I feel his cock hardening. It will be his downfall. He's not even concerned with pinning me, just thinking about fucking me.

"It was fun last time, Heartbreaker. And in another life, we'd have a fun fling, but in this lifetime, you don't get to touch me again without my say so."

I jerk on his arm, using his own weight to flip him over my shoulder. He's the smallest of the guys. Any of the others I would struggle with the move, but not with Hayes.

I don't give him time to realize what happened before I'm on top of him, pinning him to the ground.

He smiles. "I'm good with girl on top, too," he teases.

I kiss his cheek. "Keep dreaming, Heartbreaker."

Then I get off of him, not breaking a sweat.

Beckett studies me suspiciously. "Gage, you're up."

Gage walks toward the house. "You don't want to get your ass kicked by a girl?" I shout at him.

He walks back a moment later with boxing gloves. "I assume you know how to box?"

I nod, trying to hide my smile.

Gage thinks he can beat me boxing, that his upper body strength will trump mine.

I glance to Beckett, waiting for him to give some rule that will favor Gage over me.

Beckett leans back in his chair, folding his arm in front of his chest. "First to get knocked to the ground loses, even if you can still get up. Punch anywhere you want."

Gage hands me a pair of gloves and puts his on methodically, while I slip mine on quickly, getting a feel for them. I throw a couple of practice punches before Gage squares up against me.

"Ready?" he asks.

I nod.

Even though I'm only using my upper body to throw punches, boxing uses your entire body. Your punches are only as good as your footwork. And my footwork is excellent—even if the ground is uneven and I'm wearing running shoes.

Gage is more cautious than Hayes. He feels me out,

jabbing at me only once before blocking as I throw a punch. He tests my footwork, moving to force me to move.

He's good. And if we were in a boxing ring with official rules, he'd beat me hands down. But we aren't.

We both dance around a while, barely hitting each other in the face and midsection.

"My money's on Gage," Caius says.

"Ouch, even you, Charming? I thought you were on my side," I say as I duck, causing Gage to miss.

But he recovers quickly and hits me hard in the stomach. I stumble back, barely staying on my feet.

"Sorry, Princess, my money's on Gage, too," Hayes winces as I cough hard, trying to re-catch my breath.

I don't have to ask whose side Lennox is on.

Beckett is silent.

All of their responses drive me, and I know how to take Gage down. He's cautious, a careful fighter that plans out all of his moves so he doesn't get caught off guard. That may work in a ring with rounds, even ground, and official rules.

I'm still hunched over, and Gage isn't throwing a punch. He should. He should take advantage and knock me on the ground, but that's not the kind of guy he is. He's honorable.

I've caught my breath, but I don't stand all the way up. Gage is by far the biggest of the guys, has bulging muscles, and he's smart. But sometimes, that's not enough when you let your emotions in.

I run forward, like I'm going to barrel into him. It catches him off guard, just enough to mess up his stance so he won't be able to throw a full punch. He can't use his feet to knock into me, but he tries to anyway.

I let him hit my cheek. It stings, I can taste the blood,

but it allows me to get close enough to get an uppercut in and combine it with a punch to the gut. Neither are too hard, but his feet are off-balance. The ground beneath him is uneven enough that he can't recover.

Gage stumbles once, trying to stand before falling to his ass.

He blinks up at me, then smiles.

"You're good. Trained, but also had real-world fighting experience."

I nod my thanks slightly and then take off my gloves. I hold out my hand to help Gage back to his feet.

"Who's next?" I ask.

Caius pops up. "Time to get my ass kicked for betting on Gage and not you." His eyes twinkle a little.

I shake my head with a smirk, knowing there is no way he'll fight full out with me. He cares about me too much to hit me.

But we go through the motions anyway. We fight hand to hand. Punching, kicking, tackling—it's all allowed.

Caius surrenders about five minutes later after he spits blood from me knocking one of his teeth loose.

Hayes hands me a bottle of water and a towel to dry off my sweat from the sun.

"Have I earned the right to fight Len now, Hero?"

Beckett looks to Lennox. "Fight for real. Like she's the enemy. Like it's your job to kill her."

Lennox pulls out a knife and spins it around.

"If he gets a weapon, isn't it only fair that I have one too?"

"No," Beckett says.

"Aw, give her a knife. I can still kick her ass."

"No. She gets nothing."

I frown. *Is Beckett trying to get me to lose? Trying to get*

Lennox to actually hurt me? Kill me even? Has that been his plan all along?

"But—" Gage starts.

"I've made my decision. If Ri wants to back down and forfeit, she can. It's her life. There is no reward for winning." His eyes meet mine. Except there is—I gain some of his respect, his trust.

I shouldn't do this. It isn't a fair fight. I've needed saving every time the situation was real.

But that was when I forgot that I knew how to fight. I didn't think I was strong enough then, and I know differently now. I'm strong enough to be my own hero.

Lennox is good, and he won't hesitate to slice my skin. *But what's another little scar?*

My back is covered in scar tissue now. My stomach has a few.

I give my answer by running straight at Lennox, full force. He steps out of my way, like he knew I was going to do that all along.

I turn at the last second and throw a kick and a punch at the same time, knowing my best shot at winning is if I can take him down quickly before he gets a chance to use his knife.

My attack doesn't work.

He hits my head hard with his fist, harder than any of the other guys.

My head spins, and the sun looks like a thousand tiny little lights in the sky. I don't know how I stay on my feet, but I do.

And then I feel cold metal at my throat.

"Come on, Ri, you got this," Hayes says, now on my side.

"Really? You're going to bet on her?" Lennox asks.

"No, I bet on you; I just want her to at least get a punch in so we can say you got hit by a girl," Hayes teases. I feel the knife press harder against my neck until I feel a sharp sting.

The asshole sliced into my neck.

One of my arms is pinned behind my back. The other is pinned against my side as he holds the knife to my throat.

I'm facing the other guys. Hayes is leaning against a tree, still heckling Lennox. Gage looks concerned, like he's about to jump in and stop Lennox from killing me. Even Caius looks concerned and nervous, and he's barely shown any emotion since he lost his sister.

And then I see Beckett. He's looking at me sternly. He raises an eyebrow. It's the same move he did before when Jameson was attacking me. I could nod, give him an indication that I need his help, and he'd go into hero mode and save me. He does owe me one, after all.

Is that what this was about? Him setting me up so I'd have to use my hero save I earned the night before?

His jaw ticks, and I swear he winks at me, but it's so fast that maybe I imagined it.

He hasn't said whose side he's on, who he's betting on, but I think it might be me. And I'm going to give him hell for it later.

But for now, I've got an asshole to beat.

I consider my options quickly, but I know what I have to do.

I lean into the knife, until blood is oozing down my neck. I stare right at Beckett; his eyes deepen, and his teeth grind together.

I smile on the inside, seeing him in distress at my pain. His hand grips the armrest to keep himself from flying over to save me. As much as I love seeing Beckett in misery, my throat does fucking hurt as the blade slices deeper into my neck. But the pain I'm putting us both through serves a purpose.

I knock my head against his as hard as I can. Lennox is a pro, so even though he's knocked off guard, he doesn't completely release his hold like I hoped. But it's enough for me to get my arm pinned by my side free. A swift elbow to the eye has him knocked off balance.

And then it's a fight for his knife.

Lennox tries to pull it back against my throat, but I spin with his only grip on my other arm. I keep the momentum of his knife hand going, driving it right toward his heart. I only stop when the tip digs into the center of his chest.

"Yield," I demand.

Lennox grunts.

"Yield, or I'll drive this knife into your heart." I push the tip against his breastbone.

"You wouldn't."

"I would, just like you'd have sliced through the veins in my neck and not thought twice about it."

He nods, yielding to me, and I release my grip on his hand holding his knife. We look at each other a second, and I finally see the respect in his eyes. We won't be enemies anymore. We won't be besties either, but definitely not enemies.

That's when the slow clapping starts. Hayes starts, then Gage and Caius join in. Even Beckett stands with an amused grin.

I blush at the compliment.

"Can take down all of us, but she blushes when we

give her a compliment. Can you be any more incredible?" Caius says.

"I don't like compliments." I shrug, finally meeting Beckett's eyes.

His drop from amused to concerned. "We need to stitch up that wound on your neck."

I touch my neck and hold back my hiss. I forgot about the slice. I'm pretty sure it's superficial.

"I'll get the first aid kit," Lennox says, knowing that even though Beckett told him to fight me all out, he still has some making up to him to do for hurting me.

"I still have one left to fight," I say.

Beckett frowns.

Hayes laughs. "You beat all our asses. Lennox is the best fighter; if you can take him, you'll destroy Beckett."

Beckett's head snaps to Hayes, glaring at him. "And why exactly do you think that? Because I only have one arm?"

"No..." Hayes rubs the back of his neck nervously. Hair falls from the low bun he's wearing, and he's put his glasses back on, but they've fallen down his nose. He pushes them back up. "I don't mean any disrespect, but you could be the best fighter in the world, but you're at a disadvantage with only one arm to punch and defend with. Ri's a trained fighter. She knows how to take your advantage and make it your disadvantage. She's smart."

"There you go with the compliments again," I say with a huff.

Lennox jogs back with the first aid kit. Beckett takes it from him and walks over to me. He dabs at the blood with gauze and then brushes his thumb over my neck.

I purse my lips as all the air whooshes from my lungs as I stare at him staring at my wound like he cares. He cares when he shouldn't. I'm forbidden to him for so many reasons, reasons he'll never know.

"I don't think it needs stitches."

I nod.

He places a small bandage on my neck to soak up the blood. Then his hand grips my chin as he looks at me.

"You up for one more fight?" he asks, quietly.

I nod. I want to fight him, if only to be close to him.

Beckett steps back. He's in lounge shorts, and he removes his plain white T-shirt revealing his abs.

My mouth gapes.

Damn him. He knows how to knock me off-kilter. My mind is going to be locked on sex, on his glorious chest and abs, instead of focusing on how to take him down.

He smirks at my reaction.

I blow out a deep breath. This is going to be torture.

Beckett looks at Hayes, and I realize these guys have never really seen Beckett fight. They think he's weak, that I can automatically win. But this will be the most even match of the day. Whoever wins, it will be close.

"You think only having one arm is a disadvantage? Tell me after you see me fight if you still think the same," Beckett says.

The sun hits him then, and he fucking glows like a majestic god. I can't help but think he's the most beautiful man in the world. Strong muscles ripple underneath his skin. His residual limb doesn't look like a disability to me; it shows me how fucking strong he is, how much pain he's survived and has become a part of him. Just like his grief that will shape him until he comes out the other side forged anew.

When Beckett looks at me, I imagine he sees the same. My beauty, not my scars. My strength, not my pain. That's why our souls are so drawn to each other. Our pasts are similar. Our pain, our grief, our strength—it all comes from the same place.

"What are the rules?" I ask, as we begin to circle each other, preparing to fight.

"First to surrender loses."

"Style of fighting? Weapons?"

"Anything goes."

"What does the winner get?" Winning before was about earning the respect of the other guys. It was about showing Beckett that I'm not to be messed with. It was about getting him to trust me. I've done that. Winning against Beckett now won't gain me any of those things.

"Winner gets anything they want from the other."

"Horny bastards," Hayes chuckles.

Caius gives him a death glare.

Gage smiles deviously.

And Lennox says, "Their lust is going to be the death of us all."

We ignore them. There is nothing to say to it anyway. Yes, we want each other. They witnessed it last night, but that doesn't mean that we will act on those feelings. We both know what's at stake.

I try to focus on fighting Beckett. I've seen him fight before. He fought me in that box, and as far as I'm concerned, he was the clear winner, not Caius. He beat me then, and it fuels my need to beat him now. But he's not a traditional fighter. Maybe at one point, he was, but not anymore. Now he's ruthless and creative with his attacks.

I throw a punch just to see how he'll react.

He brushes it aside easily with his hand like it was a bug flying by his head.

"That all you got, Princess?" he teases.

"Nah, I just didn't want to give you a black eye. I didn't think it would look good in front of your boys, who think you're about to get beat by a girl."

His eyes roam up and down my body. "I don't see a girl here; all I see is a fighter."

I smile at that, and he takes advantage, throwing his own punch that I sidestep.

"Weak," he taunts.

I throw a quick three-punch combination. He blocks two of them, but the third hits him hard in the stomach, knocking his breath away.

"What? No comeback?" I grin.

He kicks out before he catches his breath. I try to jump back, but he's quicker, and I fall on my ass.

He's over me a second later. His glistening abs press against me while his legs straddle my waist. My hands are free, though, so I jab once while trying to catch his wrist and twisting it awkwardly until I control the movements of his arm. It takes both of my arms to hold onto his one.

I hold his arm. He has my body pinned.

"Draw?" I ask.

He laughs—a real, beautiful full-body laugh. I could bask in that sound, but instead, I take the opportunity to throw my weight, knocking him off balance until I'm on top. He catches my wrists with his one hand, though, and now we're in the same position from before but in reverse.

I frown.

He snickers. "If I was nice, I'd offer you a draw. You're good, Princess. Whatever sucker taught you did a good job, but he forgot to teach you about the monsters like me who don't fight fair."

I lean my head in confusion.

And then I feel his cock straining between my legs as his mouth lands on mine, and his tongue slips inside.

My eyes fall shut, and a deep groan rattles in my throat as he bucks his hips up, hitting that bundle of nerves between my legs.

Yes, more of that.

And then, in the next moment, I'm flipped over face first in the dirt with my arms pinned behind my back and a gun pressed to my temple.

Fuck, how could I let him manipulate me like that? And how the hell did I not realize he had a gun while I had nothing?

"What do you have to say now, Princess?" he whispers against my ear.

"You may have won, but don't think I can't pull the exact same move against you someday. You're just as susceptible to your lust as I am."

"Maybe, but there is one difference between us which will always give me the advantage—I've been burned before. Loved and betrayed. Loved and lost. It made me cynical and resistant to your charms. You are a stupid romantic, thinking I'm going to save you from this competition, marry you, and take you far away from this."

"I don't, actually."

"Then what do you want?"

"Nothing you can give me."

Beckett slowly gets off me. I roll over and stare up at him. The other guys have moved in closer and are eyeing me suspiciously. I notice that Beckett hasn't put his gun away.

I stand up cautiously, dusting the dirt off me.

"Who taught you?" Beckett asks me.

The gun isn't pointed at me, but it might as well be. He

doesn't trust me. He never will. Odette really did a number on him.

"You won't believe me if I tell you."

"I didn't ask for your opinion. I asked a question, and I expect an answer. Who taught you?"

I don't look at all their faces, only Beckett's.

"Vincent Corsi taught me."

Shock splinters through Beckett's angry glare for a split second before he regains control. I take a moment to look at all the others. All are wide-eyed, eyebrow hooked, and mouths slack. None of them believe me.

"Liar. Mafia men don't teach their daughters how to fight, especially not mafia kings. Corsi would have done anything to keep you protected, pure, and safe. That's why you have guards. Your job is to marry well. Ideally, into another mafia prince, which is why Alvise or Enrico will most likely win. This game is just for show so your father can control the rest of the gangs and elite in the area. So I'll ask you again, who are you protecting? Who taught you when they shouldn't have?"

Warm feelings wash over me as I think about all the times Vincent and I spent in his home gym. It started when I was seven; he taught me the basics. How to throw a punch. How to get out of a hold. The sensitive areas to go for. And then it became more specialized—karate, kick-boxing, how to use a knife, trips to the shooting range.

He taught me everything he could. Then he ensured I had guards at every moment, even though he knew I could defend myself, even though he knew I was better than them. They were always around, probably for show. That's what would be expected of him—protect his only daughter.

Vincent is a contradiction, and so are my feelings for

him. On the one hand, he gave me the skills to ensure I don't need a savior. I've been kidnapped too many times to count, but every time I've managed to survive, and most of the time, escape. It's because of what he taught me.

But then he tries to marry me off to a guy I don't know. He does virginity tests. He treats me like his property, and I hate him.

"You can believe me or not. But Vincent taught me how to fight, to use a knife, to fire a gun. He taught me everything himself. He didn't hire a trainer. Maybe he did that because he wasn't supposed to. Maybe he did it because he didn't have a son, and he wanted to teach me. I don't know why. I know he shouldn't have. Even being the mafia king, he was risking everything by teaching me, but he did."

I don't hate Vincent. *Why don't I hate him?* I feel like there is something I'm forgetting. Some long-lost secret that I'm not supposed to know, but I need to remember in order for everything to make sense.

Beckett is silent.

"I don't believe you, Ri. You're hiding something. You know we will do nothing but help you. We are on your side. Beckett and I are risking our lives so we can marry you. You can trust us," Caius says.

"Now who's lying? You entered the game for revenge. And yea, Caius, you're a good guy, so I'm sure if you won, you would treat me fairly as your wife, but don't act like that is why you are doing this. You think Vincent and I played a role in Odette's death, but we didn't. You can believe us or not, that's up to you. But don't feed me bullshit."

"You earned our respect, just like we've earned yours. Trust takes a long time. It would be easier if we all trusted each other. You could really help us, Ri, and we could help you, but I don't know if we can ever trust each other," Lennox says.

I nod, agreeing.

So do Gage and Hayes.

"Vincent Corsi taught you?" Beckett asks.

"Yes."

"I believe you."

Gasps fill my ears, but Beckett's words push through the distrust.

"What? Why?" Caius asks.

"She wouldn't tell us it was Corsi if it wasn't. If she's working with Corsi, which still might be the case, she would lie and say it was someone else. Telling us gives us leverage against Corsi. His men won't like that he trained his daughter. It's not the way they do things. They will see it as him trying to change how the mafia is run. Tradition is what's kept them in power all these years. If that tradition fails, they all do."

Beckett trusts me—at least a little more than he did five minutes ago. I want to talk to him alone. I want to tell him everything. My conflicting feelings about Vincent. My suspicions that I don't remember everything I should.

Also, I want to see if I can seduce him into actually fucking me. My blood rushes warm with desire, and my mouth runs dry. I want to feel him inside me. I need it, then I can let him go.

Talk, then fuck.

But I don't get the chance.

An Escalade pulls up, and a man I've never seen before pops out.

"It's Monroe. He—he had a heart attack. He's in the

hospital. He's not...he won't last long," he says after running into the backyard.

The guys all look at Caius, their eyes empathizing, but none of them speak.

"I'm sorry, Charming. I can't imagine if you lose your father after just losing your sister." I put my hand on his shoulder.

To my surprise, he turns toward me and pulls me into a hug. I wrap my arms around him tightly. He needs this—just comfort.

The hug goes on for a long time. I turn my head and see Beckett. He tries to hide his annoyance at the hug, but he can't. His jaw clenches, his hand fists.

I shoot him a look that says if he tries to interrupt this, I'm going to pummel his ass.

After several long minutes, Caius finally lets me go, but his hand finds mine, and our fingers interlock in a familiar way. It feels right just to hold his hand when he's grieving.

Hayes and Gage give him a pat on the shoulder. Even Lennox hugs him, but Caius doesn't release my hand. And I don't want him to. I hate seeing anyone in pain, in grief. I guess you would say it's my weakness. I've seen too much grief far too young.

"Should we head to the hospital then?" I ask.

Caius runs his other hand through his hair; he squeezes his eyes shut as if to block out the pain. When he opens them, his soul is back to the non-emotion he's been locked in since the loss of his sister.

"No, we have to start the initiation. It's what he would have wanted," Caius says, looking at Beckett.

"Call the others and let them know that I'm ready to

initiate, but you should be with your father at the hospital. You don't need to be at the initiation," Beckett says.

The rest of the guys fall into an awkward silence. They want to say something but won't. They move away from Caius, but not toward Beckett, as if they don't want to show support for either of them. I don't understand their actions.

"See, that's the thing. I do have to be at the initiation," Caius says.

"Why? You should be with your father," Beckett says, looking equally confused.

"The initiation rite requires a challenger. You can only win if you defeat someone, and I'm that challenger," Caius says.

13

BECKETT

CAIUS IS A SNAKE. He's not Prince Charming or whatever ridiculous nickname Ri keeps calling him. He's a foul, wicked, spineless snake.

And my assessment of him has nothing to do with how jealous I felt when Ri hugged him. She let him hold her like she belonged in his arms. She'd never let me hold her like that. She's too independent, and I'm too much of an unrighteous bastard.

It has nothing to do with how he sniffed her hair when he held her.

It has nothing to do with how he held her for way longer than was necessary to gain comfort.

It has nothing to do with how the first emotion he's shown since his sister died is lust for Ri.

It has nothing to do with anything except for one word —challenger.

No one ever mentioned a challenger. And everyone has been following my orders this entire time. But apparently, they were manipulating me because they left a very important part out. Initiation is not just some ceremony, not just some task I have to complete in front of everyone in order to get the job. No, I have to beat Caius, the current leader's son.

I've been set up, betrayed, and that's something I won't tolerate.

"What is this about challenging?"

No one looks at me as I ask the question. All the guys suddenly find the ground very entertaining.

Ri keeps her eyes going back and forth between us, but she can't mediate this.

Caius stares at me, but it's more like he's seeing through me. His emotions are once again gone.

I step into his space. If I'm going to have to beat this asshole, I'd rather beat him here and now rather than wait for some game to give him the clear advantage.

"Beckett, don't," Ri says, trying to push her hands against my shoulder to keep me back. "He just got horrible news about his father. Cut him some slack."

Her eyes are wide and pleading. Her hand is gentle yet firm on my chest. It wouldn't surprise me if she pulled a gun on me to keep me from hurting Caius.

But she does have a soft spot for him for some reason. Maybe I'm not the only one who feels a connection with her when I'm around her.

Fuck.

I step back. It's clear I'm not going to get any information from him.

"Lennox?"

He glares at me.

"Gage?"

He gives me an apologetic shrug.

"Hayes? I'll beat your ass if you don't tell me what's going on and why you fuckers didn't tell me sooner."

He adjusts his glasses and tugs loose his bun until he can run his hand through his hair.

"We should have told you, but we were forbidden."

Ri's eyes meet mine at the word. *Why the hell is everything forbidden? And why do people keep thinking that matters to me?* Nothing is forbidden to me.

"Forbidden by who?" I growl.

"Monroe and the rest of the leaders. They want a fair fight."

"How is it fair if Caius knows about the initiation, all of you did, while I knew nothing?"

"For an outsider to win, he has to defeat all of the odds. He has to prove that he is worthy of leading us."

"So everything to this point has been bullshit? You guys don't want me as your leader; you want Caius? You just fed me lies so I would go along with everything, and then what? You give me a disadvantage and let Caius kill me?"

"Unlike the mafia, we don't have our men fight to the death. Whoever loses will be offered a leadership position. You can choose any sect you want to lead. You were chosen carefully, so we're confident you'll be impactful in any part of our organization."

Chosen.

It wasn't a love story.

I'm so sick of hearing that.

It doesn't matter. It doesn't matter that they aren't really my friends; I already have friends that are my family. I even left that family because it hurt too much to see them living their happily ever afters while I had no one. Family I would have died for. Family I wasn't worthy of.

I turn to the errand boy. "Where is the initiation?"

He gives me the address. I'm surprised to see it's not the headquarters is in the city. Instead, it's a compound just out of the city. I grab my shirt and bottle of water before I march into the house to find my keys.

Everyone else enters shortly after me. Caius grabs the set of keys that goes to the SUV, and then he heads out.

I follow and head to the Maserati. It's a smaller car, but still plenty of room for someone to ride with me.

All of the guys pile in Caius's car. Ri stands at the base of the stairs that lead into the house looking back and forth between the two cars like she doesn't know which car to enter.

I furrow my eyebrow, letting her choose.

"Princess, you coming? I saved you shotgun," Caius says, rolling down the passenger window.

She flashes me one last look I can't read and then heads to Caius's car. I watch as he reaches over and takes her hand. She doesn't fight him or react. No smart words leave her mouth as far as I can tell. She just lets him hold her hand. Then she leans down and kisses the top.

I want to vomit at the sight.

Instead, I speed out of the driveway, letting the car go as fast as it can as I zip to the address.

They view me as an outsider they plucked from nowhere for Caius to defeat. They all chose him. Ri chose him. Odette picked me out to lose to him.

I don't want to be their leader, but I'm going to win. If only so I can make them all pay for destroying my life.

I was happy before.

I had a family.

But they weren't really mine. They all went home to their spouses and kids at the end of the night. When I went home, I had no one. I was alone. I'm still alone. And a lone wolf is a dangerous thing.

————

"Take your first left," the guard says as he opens the gate to the Retribution Kings' complex.

I speed up, taking my first left like he said. It's like a small city in here, complete with houses and businesses. Training facilities, the guards, the security measures—that's what makes it different from a regular town.

I stop at the last building on the street. It's a large building, and I have no doubt there is a fighting ring set up in the middle.

Caius is good, but I'm a better fighter. As long as the rules are fair. As long as he hasn't been holding back all of his skills.

But I hate being the center of attention. I hate putting on a show. My blood is boiling.

No, I don't think I'll have any problem beating him no matter the game. No matter how fair it is.

I walk inside, not sure what to expect, but I won't show fear, weakness. I won't bow to anyone.

The hallway is crowded. Most people don't notice me; they're too enthralled in their own conversations as I move past them, trying to find out what I'm expected to do. But a few of them stare. I can't hide who I am, not when I'm missing an arm.

I glare at anyone who looks. It's probably not the best way to make friends, but I don't give a fuck.

I walk toward the center room—an arena is in the middle, and all the seats surround it. We're going to be excepted to fight.

"Don't be nervous. They want you to win," a woman says next to me.

I look over at her. I've met her before, but I'm surprised she's talking to me now.

"What do you want, Emma?" She was one of Odette's best friends, but she's always made it clear that she hates me.

"Just to fill you in on what you should have been told to you from the start."

My head snaps to her. "You think I should have been told? I thought you hated me?"

"Only because I knew what marrying you would mean for Odette. She would never have a chance to find love on her own."

I frown and look back at the boxing ring.

"I'm sorry—that wasn't a reflection of you. I know you loved her. You would have loved her and taken care of her even after you found out the truth. But she deserved to be able to choose for herself."

"Odette didn't love me, did she?"

Emma bites her lip.

"Don't clam up on me now. You've always been honest. I need that right now before whatever I'm about to face."

"She didn't love you. She liked you, said the sex was out of this world hot."

I smirk.

She rolls her eyes and then chooses her next words carefully. "She might have fallen in love with you eventually, after the truth came out, after this part was all over. But Odette was young; she wasn't ready to get married. She didn't want a husband and kids yet."

I nod slowly, taking her words in.

"So I was chosen to fail, to make Caius look good."

Emma laughs. "No, not exactly. The tradition is for any of the leaders' sons to fight to become the king of the Retribution Kings."

"So why do you need me?"

"Monroe only had one son—Caius. There are three other leaders just below Monroe whose sons could compete. The first had all daughters. The second had one son, but he's better with a computer than his fists. He'd never stand a chance against Caius. And the third's son died two years ago."

I shift my feet as I wait for her to finish.

"The Kings like to think they are more evolved than the mafia, but they are all the same—sexist organizations that deem sons better than daughters. They pretend we are part of the group, while truly only thinking about us as safety risks that can be stolen to get them to do what they want. Hence why we are called Kings, not royalty or something more inclusive."

She sounds bitter about it. I look at her more closely. She's fit, and it wouldn't surprise me if she had trained to be a fighter. And yet, she will never have a shot.

"Your brother was the one who died?"

She nods, sucking back tears.

I should say I'm sorry, but after losing Odette, I'm tired of those words. They don't help.

"I'm a fool for loving her, aren't I?"

"No, that's why she chose you."

"My heart?" I scoff.

"The fact that you still had one after being in this world meant you were different. Monroe and the rest will say you were chosen because of the adversity you faced." She glances at where my arm should be. "But really, Odette found you. She liked you, thought you were hot, but also knew you would care. You would change things. Protect us in a way that Caius wouldn't. He'd stick to tradition. He'd keep things the same."

"Caius and Odette weren't on good terms?"

"They were close, and Odette loved her brother. Monroe is the exception, not the rule. Most Kings die long before they reach sixty. They marry and have kids young to ensure that someone is ready to take their place. She didn't want that for her brother."

"So, what do I do now?"

"You don't owe Odette anything. You don't owe any of us anything. But if I were you, I'd win. Then you can decide who you want revenge against—Corsi and the mafia, or Caius, Monroe, and the rest of the Retribution Kings."

I stare at her darkly.

She shrugs. "That's what they teach us all from a young age—retribution is the most important thing. It's hard to think about anything else."

I nod my head toward the ring. "I assume I'll be fighting Caius?"

"Among other things."

"Who will you be betting on winning?"

She gives me a smug smile. "Caius—everyone will be betting on Caius. He ensures our survival."

"I thought you liked me?"

"You know I've always hated you, sorry. We aren't going to be friends."

"Then, why did you tell me all of that?"

"Because Odette should have. She should have stopped the fake fairytale much sooner. You shouldn't be mourning. You should be happy you're free. Win or lose, you get to decide."

"I'm going to win."

"I hope so, but I'm still betting on Caius. He's prepared his whole life for this."

I sigh while more people file in.

"Thanks for the information, Emma. But I'd change your bet if I were you. You're not going to want to be on the wrong side when I win."

"I'm counting on it."

I don't look at her again as I jog down the stairs to where a man stands with a microphone asking people to take their seats.

"Beckett, I'm Harry, Caius's uncle."

I nod but don't shake his hand. I assume he's one of the leaders who didn't produce a son or one worth fighting, but I don't ask to confirm.

Caius walks toward us with his posse and Ri by his side.

"Harry," Caius nods at him.

"How are you holding up?" Harry asks him.

"I was born for this day."

"Good, good."

He looks from Caius to me. "We are going to do the first two steps today. The final step is more of a long game, but whoever wins the first two steps will take the leadership position from Monroe immediately. Even if he recovers, he's not in a good enough place to lead."

"What if there's a tie?" Ri asks.

"There won't be a tie," both Caius and I say at the same time in rough, gravely voices.

Harry chuckles. "There won't be a tie, but if there is, we've already accounted for that situation."

"What are the rules?" I ask.

"No rules for this first round. You fight until one of you

can't get up or surrenders. Anything goes, and any weapon you want can be brought in."

I glance to Caius, already guessing he's got a dozen weapons stashed under his clothes.

I did have the foresight to grab my gun and a knife from the car, but I don't plan on using them. My fist will do just fine.

"You both have five minutes. I'll make some announcements, and then we'll begin," Harry says.

Caius walks to the other side and starts warming up. The rest of the guys follow, although Hayes looks torn, like he might want to hang with me. But at the last minute, changes his mind and retreats to Caius's corner.

If I win, Hayes is the only one I'll give a second chance to. Everyone else can get the hell out.

"It looks like they all think Caius is going to win. What about you, Ri? Who are you betting on, Caius or me?"

"Caius..."

RI

THE GLARE BECKETT gives me when I say Caius instead of his name is priceless. I would have said Caius just to watch the smug smirk on Beckett's face turn in the devil's.

I don't think Caius is going to win; I know Beckett will. But Beckett doesn't trust me. He doesn't like me. He plays degrading games with me—games I like way too fucking much, but I'll never admit that.

If he wants me to bet on him, then he needs to be on my side too. He needs to admit he likes me, trusts me, that we are on the same side.

I lie and say Caius's name because I know it will piss Beckett off. He'll fight harder because of it to try and prove me wrong. I'll pay for it later with vicious kisses or, if I'm lucky, a delicious punish-fuck. Win-win for me.

I also say Caius's name because I need to protect my own life. Sure, I can kick a guy's ass, but not dozens. I need Caius to be willing to save me, just like Beckett is. I need him to want to win Vincent's game just like Beckett does. I can survive married to either of them—but the rest? I'd rather die.

Still, I feel bad for Beckett as I walk away, so I throw him a hint—a wink I'm not even sure he saw at first.

But then his eyes turn villainous. He looks like he wants to murder me for taunting him, for pretending to choose Caius when I'd rather choose him. I have to play my odds. Caius won't forgive me if I always choose Beckett over him. He's too sweet; his heart is too fragile.

Beckett, on the other hand, likes my snarky mouth. He likes that I'm his equal. He likes the back and forth between us.

And right now, Caius needs me more. He lost his sister; he's about to lose his father. Beckett just lost a woman he thought he loved, when really he's pissed at himself for falling for a liar.

I hear Harry start announcing the fight and rules, while the guys surround Caius, giving him a pep talk.

"You got this," I say with a smile.

"Good luck kiss?" Caius asks.

I lean forward, planning on kissing him on the cheek, when he leans forward and captures my lips before I can move. The heated stare at the back of my head tells me that Beckett sees the kiss. And Caius's smirk when he pulls away tells me he did it to piss Beckett off.

It's a mistake.

He thinks it will show that he has me. All it will do is fuel Beckett's fire more.

"You shouldn't have done that," I say.

"I wanted to."

"You wanted to piss Beckett off?"

He grabs my chin and looks deep into my eyes. "I wanted to kiss you. I've been dying to since I kissed you in the box in front of everyone. Pissing him off was just a bonus."

His eyes are sincere, and I felt him put everything into that kiss. I wish I could say I felt all the feels when he kissed me. Then I'd know that I have a chance of not having my heart broken at the end of this. Even if Beckett becomes their king, even if he wins Vincent's game, it doesn't mean he'll ever love me—not like I will him.

My only goal is to survive—but there will be no happily ever for me. There will only be hope that a man I can survive with wins, or I find a way out.

Caius hops up and into the ring, as does Beckett from the other corner. I know Caius is angry—he has plenty of pain and grief he has to work through—but he's got nothing on Beckett. I don't understand Beckett's anger, but it goes deeper than just Odette, much deeper. It's like it's been living inside him this entire time, and losing Odette allowed him to unleash it.

Hayes stands next to me, while Gage stands closer to Lennox.

"So who do you really think is going to win?" he asks so low I don't think the others heard him.

I look up at Hayes and see the twinkle in his eyes. "Apparently, the same person you do."

"Then why are you standing on this side?"

"I expect the same reason you are."

"Caius has been one of my best friends since I was five. I've never known anything else. It would be disloyal to our friendship to stand anywhere else."

"But?"

"But he was never supposed to lead. He's a good guy— too good, some would say. If he wins, it will destroy him. He needs Beckett to win as much as Beckett does."

"Why?"

He shakes his head. "It's not my place to say, and Caius

will never admit it, but he'd be better off as one of the leaders, not the king."

I chuckle when he says king. "King? Really? You guys will truly act like Caius or Beckett is royalty when one of them wins?"

"Don't act like the mafia is any different, Princess."

"Touché."

We both give our full attention to the fight as it begins. I should be nervous. Two men I care about are about to duke it out. Even if I want Beckett to win, I'm still worried about what losing will do to Caius. But I'm not nervous; I know the outcome already.

The fight starts, and Caius throws the first punches, eager to win. Beckett is far more patient and far more deadly. He could simply wait for Caius to tire himself out throwing punches and then make his move. But Beckett is far too angry to let it get that far.

Beckett throws me a look, and I offer him a raised eyebrow like he's done so many times to me. This time my raised eyebrow isn't one of me offering to help him. It's one that says, *really, you're just going to let him dance around you like that and not fight back?*

Beckett's nostrils flare as he looks back at Caius. And then he attacks and attacks and attacks.

I've never seen him so angry, so determined, so one-track focused.

They are allowed to use weapons; there are no rules. But the way Beckett is attacking—he doesn't need anything but his fist and determination to prove everyone wrong.

"What did you do?" Lennox asks me.

"What did I do? I'm right here."

Lennox scoffs. "Your kiss wasn't enough; you had to go and taunt him from the sidelines, too?"

I fold my arms across my chest. "It's not my fault if Beckett kicks Caius's ass. If things were fair, I would have been on Beckett's side. The fact that not one of you offered to stand next to him just shows what asses you all are. You lied to him repeatedly. When he wins, don't think he's going to let you anywhere near his inner circle. You'll be lucky to remain part of the Retribution Kings."

"Don't you think we know that! We don't have a choice. We vowed loyalty to Caius when we were kids. We are loyal to him until he loses. Then we will have to grovel if Beckett doesn't kill us first," Lennox says.

I narrow my eyes. "So you think Beckett is going to win?"

"Of course, he's going to win. But now, because of you, he's probably going to kill Caius instead of just knock him out."

I look back, and sure enough, Caius is on his knees, covered in blood. He should surrender, but Beckett doesn't give him the opportunity. He pummels into him over and over. Caius's head cracks as blood spews.

I gasp and that gets Beckett's attention.

He frowns.

Please, I plead with my eyes. *He's had enough.*

Beckett sighs. I don't think he'll listen to my pleading. But he hits him one more time in the head, and Caius collapses to the floor.

Silence stretches through the room. It's not exactly a surprised gasp, more like everyone knew this was inevitable, but they aren't sure how they feel about the outcome. I have no doubt that if Caius had won, there would be cheering.

Harry walks back to the ring, holds up Beckett's hand, and announces him as the winner. Blood oozes from his knuckles, a bruise surrounds his left eye, and sweat drenches his forehead and shirt. Eventually, people start clapping for him.

Gage, Lennox, and Hayes rush onto the stage to pick up Caius and drag him off.

Beckett stares at me.

I want to run to him.

I want to congratulate him. Hug him. Kiss him. Fuck him.

I want...

It doesn't matter what I want. Beckett isn't mine. He doesn't want me. He wants to torment me.

Instead, I give him a small nod of congratulations before Caius is dragged to where I stand. His eyes roll in his head as Gage pours water over his face. Eventually, Caius looks at me with half his eye hanging out of his socket and a badly bruised and cut-up lip.

"Don't look so concerned, Princess. The next round is an obstacle course. One I've practiced a thousand times. I'll win," Caius says, and then he kisses my hand before falling unconscious again.

I look to the other guys, and they look ashamed.

Shit.

Caius is going to cheat. He already knows he'll win the next round. I have no idea what the tiebreaker is. I like Caius a lot, but Beckett needs to win. I need him to win everything. Caius may be my Prince Charming, but Beckett's my Hero. Charming looks great in a tux and can dance at the ball, but only a true Hero will be by my side to fight the darkest monsters.

I have to tell Beckett.

15

BECKETT

I won, but she stayed by his side.

I've had enough. If she thinks this will make me trust her more, she's crazy. She chose him; she thinks he's the better between the two of us.

She's right, of course. Caius has never betrayed or hurt her. I'm the bad guy—the one who's embarrassed her and used her desires against her. I'm the one who started this war. Caius wants nothing more than to sweep her off her feet and go riding off into the sunset in a horse-drawn carriage ride.

While I want...fuck, I can't admit what I want.

This isn't about Odette anymore.

It's about Rialta.

I want her.

She's mine.

Not Caius's.

Not any of those men competing for her.

Mine.

What I'm going to do with her when I win her, I'm not

really sure. I just want her—on her knees, in my bed, by my side.

Except she's a manipulative liar, just like everyone else.

I thought I was beginning to trust her. I thought that someday maybe I'd fully trust her.

And then she chooses him.

After Harry announces me as the winner, I walk off.

"Beckett," he snaps as I jump out of the ring.

I turn my head just enough to signal that I'm listening.

"Seven PM, round two, at the course near the back of this building."

I nod, and then I get the hell out of there. I need space to clear my head. I need fuel for the next competition.

I've barely hopped in my car, and my foot is already on the gas, speeding out of my parking spot. I don't know where I'm going. If it was up to me, I'd drive and drive and drive. I'd go find some guy to fight. I'd drink myself until I couldn't think anymore.

But that's not what I'll do now. I drive until I find a local restaurant, still within the confines of the Retribution Kings' compound, and then I force myself out of my car and into a booth. I order carbs. I guzzle down glasses of water.

I don't think. I shut off my mind.

My only goal is to win the next round. After that, I'll have all the power. Then I can decide what to do, what I even want anymore. *Who do I want retribution from? Who do I need?*

I'm digging into pasta when Ri walks in. She's wind-blown and out of breath, like she ran the whole way here. She probably did, unless Caius let her take the car.

She spots me instantly, straightens her face, wipes the flyaways from her face, and then marches over to me.

"No," I say between bites when she stops at my booth.

She looks at the seat across from me and then slides in anyway.

I glare at her.

"You chose the loser's side; that means you get to eat with him, not me."

"Caius was taken to the hospital to ensure he doesn't have a concussion."

"Then why aren't you by his side, holding his hand while he gets an x-ray?"

"I'm waiting for my thank you," she leans back, folding her arms across her chest as the waitress approaches.

"What can I get you, sweetheart?"

I scoff. "She's not a sweetheart."

The waitress ignores my comment.

"A burger and fries."

"If anything, you owe me a thank you, not the other way around. I'm not paying for your burger and fries," I snark.

She reaches into her pocket, pulls out a twenty, and throws it at me.

"Now, about my thank you," she says, still waiting.

"You betrayed me. Why should I thank you?"

"You're a real ass, you know that?"

I shovel in more food even though my stomach wants to stop because of this conversation. I'm going to need the fuel this evening, so I force myself to keep eating.

"You're supposed to thank me for helping you win."

"And how exactly did you do that? I don't remember you throwing any punches out there."

"I taunted you, pissed you off, gave you extra fuel, an extra reason to go after Caius."

I growl.

She smiles. "You look like the beast in Beauty in the Beast, barely using your silverware as you shovel food in with a sexy growl."

I shake my head. "Is that what you came here to say to me? I look like a cartoon character?"

"No, the live-action version."

I stop eating and stare at her. I swear I'm going to murder her someday.

"Why are you here, Ri? I want to eat and clear my head before the next round, and I don't want to deal with your treasonous ass right now."

Her shoulders slump at my words, and she sighs. "Fine, I'll leave." She stands up. "But if you think I chose Caius because I think he's better than you, you're wrong."

The waitress chooses that moment to bring her food out.

Ri picks up the burger, takes one giant bite, and then plucks a couple of fries before she starts to walk away. She returns a second later with a poorly wrapped peanut butter cup.

"I always choose you, Hero."

And then she walks away, leaving me thoroughly confused.

Why the hell did she just give me a peanut butter cup? And why is the only image playing in my head the one of her taking a bite of the burger while juices ran down her chin?

I shake it off and finish my meal, ignoring the peanut butter cup.

I pay.

I leave.

I sit in my car, trying to nap before the competition, the peanut butter cup staring at me on the dash.

I sigh and finally unwrap it. The chocolate has started to melt, but I pop it in my mouth in one go.

It tastes like cheap chocolate and stale peanut butter. It was probably expired.

I'm about to crumple the wrapper up, when I see handwritten words on the inside.

———

Caius is going to cheat.

———

I stare at Ri's words. *Why didn't she just tell me?* I didn't give her a chance, and that restaurant was crawling with people who belong to the Retribution Kings. Any one of them could have tipped off Caius.

She helped me.

She wants me to see that she's on my side, but all I see is that she's playing all sides. She's hedging her bets, ensuring that she doesn't end up on the losing side.

I don't trust her. I don't trust anyone. I can't ever again.

But her words rattle around in my head, "I always choose you, Hero."

The words try to go deeper, try to penetrate my heart. I won't let them. I won't let her. She should choose Caius. He might actually choose her in return.

I'll only choose retribution.

———

I arrive at seven on the dot. No reason to get here early. No reason to stand around while everyone stares at me.

I expect it to be another fight, or maybe a shoot-off or weapons skills test.

Instead, we are at the back of the property with what looks like an obstacle course.

My arm twitches. I'm strong, and I know how to compensate for my lost arm in most circumstances, but those monkey bars look like a bitch.

Caius is sitting on the end of some bleachers, with Hayes and Gage next to him. Lennox is behind him, massaging his shoulders. But I don't see Ri.

I frown.

I should approach and ask them where she is, but she's probably just sitting in the sea of faces in the bleachers. Or she ran off to get Caius water or painkillers or something.

Caius turns in my direction, and I see his swollen black and blue face with stitches on his cheek.

I resist the urge to smirk. Ri calls him charming, and I'm sure he is, but I hope she changes his nickname to lying, cheating bastard; that seems more fitting. I haven't figured out what to do with the info Ri gave me. It's not like she gave me any specifics. And calling him out in front of people he grew up with and consider him family isn't going to win me any loyalty.

Harry is standing at the base of the bleachers, where the course seems to start. He turns to greet me as I approach.

"I've already explained the rules to Caius," Harry says to me.

Sure, he didn't explain it to him years ago and had him practice every day growing up. I'm sure he just told him out of the blue when he showed up.

"The course should take about two hours to complete."

I glance behind him, not seeing how it will take us that long.

"It goes through the nearby forest, and there are some unmarked areas."

Of course, there are. That's how he'll cheat.

My hand fists, and the veins in my arm bulge.

He looks at my missing arm. "I can offer you a head start or modifications for certain elements—"

"No, I'm fine." I don't care that I only have one arm. I don't care that Caius is going to cheat. I don't care that the odds are stacked against me.

"Then take your place at the starting line," Harry says with a smile. I don't know if his grin is because he knows I'll lose or because he wants a leader like me—who, when the odds are stacked against them, will fight and win anyway.

Caius walks up next to me, stretching his arms.

"How's your head?" I snicker.

He smiles. "You can't goad me, Beckett. I know you're a better fighter than me. It doesn't mean that you're prepared for this course."

"Because you're going to cheat?"

"There are no rules, so there is no way to cheat."

A gun fires, and Caius takes off. I run a bit slower after him, knowing this is going to come down to pacing and who can maneuver through the forest section better as the sun begins to set.

I climb over the climbing wall easily, just behind Caius. I run through tires, dive under barbed wire, and then I get to the damn monkey bars. Caius flies through them, knowing it's going to take me a lot longer on this part than it should.

I grab the first rung, swing my body back and forth to

get momentum, and then fling myself as far as I can, hoping I can catch the next rung. I do, but my shoulder throbs from my weight when I catch myself. But I can do it.

It takes me five swings to get across, but I do.

Caius is long gone, already headed into the woods.

I glance behind me one more time, looking for her dark eyes to give me a wink, a taunt, something to drive me, but Ri's not there. I don't find her. That magnetic pull isn't there. There is a sinking feeling in my gut that something's wrong.

I ignore my concern; Ri can take care of herself. She's a fighter. This complex is impenetrable. She's safe here from outsiders, and no one here would hurt her.

I jog into the woods, and then I curse like hell. Caius is going to win.

The wood section of the obstacle course is just that—woods. Trees, shrubs, thorns, rocks. There's a very faintly marked path with a ribbon tied around branches far too spaced out for me to not make several wrong turns.

When I finally make it back to the bleachers, I know I've lost. I'm exhausted; my body is scratched from the branches, the bottom half of my legs are covered in mud. And I want to kill Caius because he's sitting on the front row in pristine condition. He definitely didn't just take the same path I did.

I don't ignore him this time. I walk straight to him and the guys, needing to find Ri. She's all I thought about. The sinking feeling is getting worse with each step.

"Where's Ri?" I ask, looking from Caius, to Gage, to Lennox, then Hayes.

They all look sick, even Caius, but none of them answer me.

"Where's Ri, Hayes?" I know he's the one most likely to crack.

"Taken."

"What do you mean she's taken? And why are we playing this stupid initiation game if someone's taken her?" I say through clenched teeth, trying to get as much information before I lose my cool and chase after her.

"Harry took her. It's for the tiebreaker. He figured there would be one, so he snatched her," Hayes says.

"Snatched her? As in, she didn't go willingly?" I ask, about to murder everyone here.

"We've been looking for her while you two were competing, but she's not on any of the security feeds. I have no idea where she is or who Harry had take her," Gage says.

"Fuck!" I yell. Heads turn toward us, but I don't care.

Harry walks over. "The tiebreaker is the first one to find and save the girl."

"What do you mean, 'save?'"

He pulls out his phone with a smirk. "It means you have one hour. If you don't find her, she dies."

I blink, not believing I heard him correctly. "What do you mean she dies? Corsi will kill us all if we don't bring her back."

"There was division in the leadership about if we should play Corsi's game to ensure we take out everyone who had anything to do with Odette's death or just do the obvious, easy thing: kill Rialta. A princess for a princess, so to speak."

"That will start a war you're not going to win. Corsi is prepared. He has his men ready, while we're fighting over who is going to lead."

Harry shakes his head. "We are always ready for war. We aren't scared of Corsi or any of the mafia. And we will have our leader decided by tonight." He glances at his watch. "You have fifty-three minutes until she dies."

I grab his shirt, and to my surprise, every one of the guys behind me points his gun at Harry's head.

"I'm only going to ask this once; where is Rialta?" I ask.

"You won't shoot me. If you do, there will be retribution, a price on your head," Harry laughs.

I look behind me; Caius is standing with his gun pointed at Harry, the same as the others.

"Caius and I may not agree on much, but we both want Rialta alive. So tell me where she is, or we'll kill you, and no matter which one of us wins, there will be no retribution for your death. We will both gladly kill you to save her."

I tighten my grip, cutting off his breath. When he gets the message, I loosen my hand enough for him to talk.

"Then, I guess I'll die for the cause. I'd rather die this way than from a heart attack like Monroe."

And then someone fires, and Harry's head falls limp in my hand.

I look to my left, expecting Hayes to be the one to shoot; I think he likes Ri the best. But it's not him. It doesn't seem like Gage or Caius shot either, but neither seems broken up about Harry's death.

"Lennox?" I ask.

He shrugs, holstering his gun. "I've wanted to shoot him for years. Glad to have finally gotten orders to do it."

"Technically, neither of us gave orders," I say, looking to Caius.

"I did," Caius says. "Or at least, I'll say I did." He looks around at the crowd that doesn't seem heartbroken that Harry is now lying on the ground in a puddle of his own blood. "And the bystanders will back me up. Emma was all he had left, and she hated him. He wanted to die."

I start digging through his pocket for his phone to see if he called anyone to take Ri. "How much time do we have left?"

"Forty-nine minutes," Hayes says.

We all look at him. "I started a timer as soon as he said we have an hour."

I look to Caius. "Are we working together or still competing?"

"It's Ri, whatever it takes to find her as fast as possible," he answers.

I nod.

We are only doing this to prevent a war, not because any of us have any sort of feelings for her.

"Knowing Ri, she's already talked her captors' heads off, disarmed them, and cut off their balls. So everyone, relax," Lennox says.

We all know he's probably right, but that doesn't ease any of our tension.

"Where do we start? Who wasn't here that should have been?" I ask.

"Harry's guards," Gage says.

I frown. "His guards?"

"We are Caius's. We swore an oath when we were five, then renewed the vow at sixteen and marked our skin with tattoos of Caius's crown. He will be a king, a leader of our group, whether he is the king or just one of many.

There are five kings in our group and one who is king of everything. Monroe is the current king. The rest are more like princes. All of them have three guards who vow to protect and be their right-hand guys. We are Caius's," Hayes says.

And then it all makes sense. They couldn't choose me even if they wanted to.

"So when I become a prince or king...?"

"Then you will choose three to guard you."

"But not you three?"

Silence.

"No, they are mine. You would have to choose others," Caius says with a growl.

Interesting.

"So Harry's guards most likely have her. How do we find them?"

Gage snatches Harry's phone from my hand, and he starts typing furiously.

"They won't be on the grounds," Hayes says.

"No, I suspect they will be somewhere about an hour away. Harry wanted her dead; that much was clear," I say.

"The lake, then," Caius says.

We all look at him.

"A boat on the lake. It would be the hardest to track, to get to," he finishes.

Our faces drop.

Gage nods his head. "They took her to the lake. They don't have reception, so I can't pinpoint where exactly, just the dock they launched the boat from."

Fuck!

We all start running toward our cars. "When we get there, I want everyone in different boats. We all take a slightly different direction, radio will be turned to station two to communicate if we see her, and shoot no matter your relation to them."

"Agreed, I'll go north, Beckett you go northeast, Hayes east, Lennox northwest, and Gage west," Caius says.

I make it to my car first, expecting the others to ride with Caius again, but Hayes jumps into the passenger seat as I take off. He gives me directions as I drive the fifteen minutes to the pier twenty over the speed limit. That leaves about thirty to find her in the lake.

I run a red light, horns honk, but I just keep driving.

"We're going to find her. And like Knox said, she's probably already escaped, tied them up, and is driving the boat this way," Hayes says, trying to reassure me.

I see Caius's car behind me as I pull up to the dock.

"Gage has already arranged for five boats," Hayes says.

I've barely put the car in park before I'm running down the gravel toward the dock. I grab the first boat and have it started and pulled out before I glance behind me. Every guy has moved just as quickly. They are all pulling out into the lake.

We're going to find her. It won't be too late.

It depends on my definition of too late. She should have never been taken. And I don't know if they will torture her, rape her, hurt her before they kill her.

The boats are small speedboats that are made for five people, so with only one, they fly.

It's a busy holiday weekend, though, so there are boats fucking everywhere.

It's easy to spot the tourists and party-goers, though. Their music blasts loud enough that I don't even bother going near any but the silent ones to get a closer look.

I glance at my phone every few minutes, watching the seconds tick by.

I turn on the radio. "Anything?"

"No sign yet," Gage answers.

"Me neither," Hayes says.

"I've found a suspicious acting boat. Keeps driving aggressively anytime I try to get near. It could be them," Caius says.

"Send us your coordinates," I say.

"I'm closest; I'll go," Lennox says.

I keep driving, but I want to go meet them. If she's there, I need to see with my own eyes. I need to kill every fucker on that boat.

But something deep in my gut tells me to keep going, just a little further.

I keep going forward, listening carefully to the radio in case Caius finds her.

Then I see a boat. No lights on. No music. A boat that looks like it's trying to hide in the evening dusk. My heart trembles, and I know it's her.

Am I too late?

16

RI

MY SHOULDER THROBS as I try to figure out how to get the engine started again. I'm pretty sure the bastards disabled it somehow. Cut the gas line. Emptied the fuel. Dropped the anchor. I don't know, but they did something to make sure that even if I did escape and kill them that I would be stuck in the middle of nowhere with no way to get off unless I want to swim the couple of miles to shore or take my chances with one of the drunk party boats that occasionally come by.

Also, based on the water filling the bottom of the boat, I'm pretty sure I'm sinking.

"Great, just great," I mutter under my breath as I try to get the motor started again. I put my entire body into it and fall against the side of the boat into my dislocated shoulder.

"Fuck," I groan.

But I don't get to revel in my misery long. I see the shadow even in the darkness.

There were three men. I killed them all.

Did I miscount?

Did I forget one?

This boat isn't that big. I don't know where one would have been hiding. It took me a while to find the third guard, so maybe he called for help before I killed him.

My gun is in the back of my leggings. In one motion, I spin, aim, and fire.

The guy ducks and chuckles. "Good thing I knew you were going to shoot and ask questions later, or I'd be dead. Your aim is good."

"Beckett?"

He smiles, and the moonlight catches the white of his teeth. Without thinking, I run toward him and throw my one good arm around him, dropping my gun.

I expect him to push me away; he doesn't. His arm wraps around me, holding me so hard against him that I can feel the speed of his beating heart against mine.

"You came."

"Well, I owed you a hero save."

I frown. "I'm not sure this counts since I killed them all myself."

He chuckles. "Then what are you doing sitting on a boat in the middle of the lake for?"

I sigh. "I couldn't figure out how to get the boat started."

"You fought off how many men?"

"Three."

"Were you tied up?"

"Yes, I had to purposefully dislocate my shoulder to get out of the ties."

"So you dislocated your shoulder to escape being tied up, found a gun, and killed three dangerous men all on your own, but you couldn't figure out how to get the boat to start?"

I nod, thankful that it's too dark for him to see my embarrassment.

"Then I'm definitely counting this as a rescue mission. We're even after this."

"That's just because you want me to do something embarrassing again, or you want to fuck me without telling me you want me."

His eyes darken as he holds me closer. "When I fuck you, I'm doing that because I want to."

When I fuck you.

Those words have me salivating.

He smirks. "But I'm not fucking you when you have a dislocated shoulder, and there are four other guys worried to death about you. Plus, I'm still pissed you took Caius's side."

"I didn't take Caius's side, you asshole. I knew you'd win. I wanted you to win. But I have to look out for myself. You'll forgive me for not choosing you. Caius won't."

"How do you know I'll forgive you?"

"Because you have before."

His eyebrows turn downward, and his lips thin. But his grip on me doesn't loosen.

"I should teach you how to drive a boat, but then you might not need my hero services. Then, I might not have an opportunity to get what I want from you."

I almost tell him he can take whatever he wants from me for free, but then I remember that I need him as much as he needs me. I have to manipulate him into rescuing me since he's still stuck on his ex, even though she never loved him. He has trust issues, he'll always have trust issues, and I don't have a say in whom I'm with anyway.

Beckett helps me into his boat, radios in that he found me, and tells the guys to meet us back at the dock.

I wince when he sets me down.

"Want me to fix that shoulder now or later? Either way, I'll make sure the guys know what a badass you are," Beckett says with a wink.

"Fix it now. And I don't need your help to get the others to like me."

"No, I'm sure they fell for you the second you let them stick their cocks in you," he says in a deep, jealous voice.

"Jealous? I'm pretty sure I made you the same offer, but you turned me down."

"I don't share, Princess."

"I don't either, Hero."

We stare into each other's eyes. Out of nowhere, Beckett grabs my shoulder, spins me around so that my back is to his front, and plants a hard, wet kiss on my lips. It's the kind of kiss that hits deep into my bones. It vibrates around in my body until my muscles tremble with desire. His kiss is delicious and intoxicating. His tongue sweeps in like he owns my mouth. He does. No man has ever kissed me like he does.

I don't think anything can bring me out of the dream that is this kiss. I'm wrong, though. The pop of pain in my shoulder shatters my bliss.

"Fuck," I say, grabbing my shoulder and bending over.

"Don't act like my kiss wasn't better than any painkiller."

He's right. I'd prefer his kisses to any drug.

"Come here." He holds out his hand to me.

I take it, and he pulls me to the steering wheel. "This is called a steering wheel."

"I know that, asshole."

He chuckles. "This is the throttle. This is the ignition. Speedboat 101. Push this, then turn this, and you'll go."

"I did, and the other boat didn't go."

"That's because you flooded the engine by trying too fast. You have to ease into it."

He puts his hand over mine and shows me how to increase the speed slow and steady. He gives me a couple of other tips as we drive back.

When we get to the dock, he doesn't have time to give me a lesson in how to park the boat or tie it off. All the guys are running toward me. I can see their relieved expressions even though the only light is the shine of the moonlight.

Lennox reaches me first.

"Careful," Beckett warns, slowly releasing me as Lennox throws his arms around me.

My eyes widen in stunned silence as Lennox hugs me. I try to turn around and look at Beckett to understand why the man who has shown his dislike for me the most is the first to hug me.

"You're alive," Lennox says, relieved.

"I am. Why are you hugging me?"

"Because I thought we'd find you dead, just like Odette."

My heart aches for him. I always forget that the others knew Odette too. They hurt too.

"Did you kill them?" he asks, holding my shoulders as he looks at me. It kills my hurt shoulder, but I don't say anything.

"Yes."

"Good, I killed Harry for you."

I smile softly, trying to keep the tear that's forming in my eye. "Thank you."

"Stop hogging her," Hayes says, grabbing me next and engulfing me in a hug as he picks me off the floor.

"Careful," Beckett growls.

"I have ice. Where are you hurt?" Gage asks, holding up a back of ice.

"Her shoulder," Beckett grabs the bag of ice. "She had to dislocate it to get out of the ties."

"Badass," Gage says, giving me a quick pat on the back as Beckett holds the ice to my other shoulder.

And then Caius is in front of me. "I'm—I'm so sorry, Ri. I suspected, but I should have never done the obstacle course until I knew you were safe. I just assumed you were in the stands and didn't want to choose sides. My uncle, Harry...I'm sorry. I didn't think he'd try to kill you."

I reach out my hand to his cheek. "Don't apologize. It's not your fault. You didn't know."

"But it was my family. When I realized they took you, when I realized they threatened your life, that you might be...I'm sorry. I should have protected you. It was my job to protect you. I was too worried about the initiation and beating Beckett that I risked your life. You didn't deserve it. You have enough you're already dealing with. When you are with the Retribution Kings, you should be safe."

I pull him into a hug, knowing he needs it. His heart thumps faster, just like Beckett's did when I hold him. His words were sweet, honest, vulnerable—things I'll never get from Beckett.

I kiss his neck, and he buries his head in my hair. I feel a tear sliding down his cheek that he brushes away quickly.

Finally, I step back.

Everyone is staring at me, but no one speaks.

"Here," Beckett says, releasing the bag of ice. I hold it up to my shoulder on my own, realizing that when I was hugging Caius, Beckett was still holding the ice to my back.

"So, who won?" I ask a moment before realizing my big mouth shouldn't have said anything.

"Beckett won the fight, as you know. Caius won the obstacle course. Finding you was supposed to be the tiebreaker, but we all formed one team to find you. We didn't care about the stupid initiation competition anymore," Gage says.

I look between Caius and Beckett. That's all good and well, but someone has to win. There can only be one leader—one.

"Beckett won," Caius says at the same time Beckett says, "Caius won."

"You're part of the Retribution Kings since birth. You want this. You have your team. You should lead them," Beckett says.

Caius shakes his head. "I wanted it because I wasn't sure an outsider was better. But Odette didn't want me to lead; she wanted you. She believed in you. And you were the one to find Ri. You saved her, not me."

"She saved herself," Beckett says.

"Does that mean—" I start.

"No," Beckett says to me, interrupting my question about him still owing me a save.

A smile tugs at my lips.

"You deserve to lead. You're better at it. More experienced. Odette wanted it. You're better at protecting Ri than I am. The guys will follow you until you find your own guards. The only reason there even was a tiebreaker is because I cheated during the obstacle course. If I hadn't, you probably would have won, and then there would have been no reason for them to take Ri. You won, Beckett," Caius says.

Beckett just nods.

And then he looks to me. Beckett may have won, but that doesn't mean he's won me. He would if I had any say in it, but Vincent chooses. Even if I could choose, Beckett still wouldn't pick me.

"We need to go back to tell everyone what happened, so you can gain temporary control until my father...until you finish your final task of getting retribution," Caius says.

We all walk down the dock toward the cars. Caius breaks off to one car, Beckett to the other. The other guys seem as torn as I am about which car to ride in.

When I look at Beckett, I know where I want to be and I'm tired of hiding my feelings. Caius made it clear he's sorry. He owes me, even if I pick Beckett.

I walk to the passenger seat of Beckett's car. I watch as Hayes follows, but Beckett shakes his head at him. Hayes laughs as he jumps in Caius's SUV.

Beckett starts driving. I lean my head back, resting the bag of ice on my shoulder, knowing it's going to take a few days for the ache to go away.

"What now?" I ask Beckett.

"You heard Caius. I have to go back to claim my throne."

I smile when Beckett says 'throne.'

"It wouldn't surprise me if there was an actual crown and throne. They seem to take their rituals seriously."

"You're probably right."

"But that's not what I meant. I meant you're going to be their leader, and then what? Do you still want to lead them after what they did? Do you still want retribution for

Odette? Or do you want to forget everything and go back to your life before? Start again?"

We pull up to the Retribution Kings' headquarters. He stops the engine and looks deep into my eyes. "I don't have a choice. Neither of us has a choice. And if you think either of us does, you're more naive than I thought." He gets out of the car and walks around to my side, helping me out. "Stay close. We won't stay long, just long enough for them to recognize me as their leader."

I nod.

He cups my chin and then kisses me softly on my lips. "We may not have a choice about our future, but tonight we have a choice."

I cock my head, not understanding.

He smirks. "I want to make a new deal. I fuck you for a lifetime of me saving you."

17

———

BECKETT

I GRAB Ri's hand attached to her uninjured arm and don't plan on letting it go—ever if I had my choice, but at least until I have her safely away from these people. Even some in the Retribution Kings apparently hate her and want her dead. I won't let anyone hurt her ever again.

As we start walking back into the building that Caius and I fought in, I feel the other guys surrounding us. For once, I truly know that they are on our side—even Caius.

It's much quieter than before, but people are still milling about even though it's the middle of the night. They're no doubt waiting to find out who their new leader is. They eye us as we walk in, and it should be clear from my position in the front of the group that I won. A man approaches us as we walk down the stairs to the ring.

"So we have a winner?" he asks with a happy smirk.

My eyes darken, and I grip Ri's hand so tight I'm sure I'm breaking bones.

"We do. I won, but if anyone pulls a stunt like that again, I'll kill them. I don't care who they are to this organization. You wanted me as your leader, you got me," I say.

185

The man's eyebrows jump up as he looks from me to Caius. I can see him nod sternly in agreement out of the corner of my eye. The man's smile gets brighter as if he's happy I won.

"Come, Beckett, you and I have a lot to talk about. I'm Charles, by the way," he says, holding his hand out.

"Actually, we don't. It's been a long night." I tuck Ri under my shoulder. "All I want is to confirm I'm the leader. I won't have any more trouble, and now I'm going to bed."

"Of course. Let me just introduce you as the winner first. You'll have to say a few vows, and then you can go."

"No crown? No blood oath?" I snarl.

He laughs. "We'll save that for the full initiation later after you get retribution."

I roll my eyes. I was joking, but apparently, he isn't.

"Did you take care of Harry's body?" Caius asks.

"We did. And unless Beckett here wants us to get retribution for his death...," he pauses, waiting for my answer.

"Harry got what he deserved," I answer.

"Good, then that's settled."

We follow Charles down the stairs to the center ring. Ri shivers at the ring. It surprises me since she's spent her entire life on a pedestal, all eyes on her.

I help her up in the ring, not allowing a break in our hands. Caius, Gage, Lennox, and Hayes join us as well.

Charles grabs a microphone, and the room silences.

"It's late, and everyone wants to sleep, so I'll make this short. We have a winner, a new leader, a new king. Beckett is the winner."

The crowd breaks out into loud cheers and applause.

My eyes roam the room, trying to understand this new group, of which I just became the leader. The applause isn't because they are happy that I'm their new leader. Some may be genuinely happy, but others are only clapping out of self-preservation. They know that I have the power to kill them without fear of retribution.

"Beckett will assume temporary control that will become permanent after he gets retribution for Odette." Charles turns to me. "Do you, Beckett, vow to be loyal to the Retribution Kings? Do you promise to protect everyone who pledges loyalty to the Kings—man, woman, and child? Do you vow to do everything in your power to put the interests of the group first when leading? And most importantly, do you vow to get retribution for anyone who breaks our trust, our loyalty, or is in any way our enemy? Do you accept that if you fail to uphold your vows, you will pay with your life?"

The room is silent as they wait for my answer.

Monroe is the oldest king there has ever been. It doesn't take a history lesson to understand why. Their enemies killed them; or they failed to uphold their vows, and their own people killed them. Either way, it's not a long job.

I look out into the crowd, knowing this moment is important. I already know I'm going to break the vows. I don't care about any of them. Tried to hurt me, but I won't let them do it again.

With ice-cold vengeance, I say, "I vow to be the greatest king you've ever known."

The crowd cheers once again.

I don't wait around to hear more. I tug on Ri's hand, and then we are running up the stairs and out the back door. We jog quickly out of the building and back to my car. I don't wait for the others. Unfortunately, I have to release Ri's hand to be able to drive the car, and I feel empty and lost the second that I do.

I drive and drive.

Away from this horrible place.

Away from the guys I don't know if I should trust or not.

Away from it all.

Ri hasn't spoken. She hasn't asked any questions, but when she sees that we aren't driving back to the cabin, she finally speaks up.

"I'm not sure what your new deal means," she says, her voice soft, timid, so unlike her.

My eyes cut to her. She's cradling her sore arm, shivering slightly in her seat.

I flick on her heated seat, and her dark eyes engulf me.

"We're going to your apartment," I say because I know she's wondering.

"I guessed that when you turned back toward the city. That or you're returning me to Vincent because I'm nothing but trouble."

"I'm not returning you. You aren't his. You're mine," I say.

"You keep saying that." She tugs on her seatbelt, adjusting herself in the seat. "But I can't be yours."

"It's true, though. There's the stupid game. Your father. The Retribution Kings. All our enemies. My old family. But none of them matter. You're mine. You belong to me."

"What if I want to belong to myself?" she whispers.

I stop the car in the parking lot next to her apartment. I turn slowly in my seat so I can face her.

"I'd call you a liar." My thumb strokes against her neck, and she gasps. "You don't want to belong to yourself. You want to belong to me. You want me to want you in all ways. To love you, marry you, die for you. You want the fairytale, the hero to come save you from this life you were born into, even though you're fully capable of saving yourself. Your life may not have dragons and moats, but you're trapped in a tower all the same. You want to be mine."

She closes her eyes as I kiss along her neck, pulling soft moans from deep inside her. She tilts her head back, giving me better access until I nip on her earlobe, and she almost falls apart. But then her eyes snap open, and she grabs my wrist, stopping me from stroking her neck again.

"You're wrong."

"I'm not."

"You are." Her lips hover over mine, and her tongue darts out, tracing a line along her bottom lip. "I don't want to be yours, unless you're also mine. And you'll never be mine. You'll never open yourself up again to belong to anyone. Belonging to someone isn't a weakness; it's a vulnerability. It's risking everything. Odette hurt you too badly to ever belong to anyone ever again."

She pulls back, and then there is far too much space between us. But damn, she's right. I hate that she's right.

I've lost too much already. If I hadn't, I would go after Ri full-hearted. I would do everything to win her, to defeat her father, to take her far away from here, somewhere where she's safe. Somewhere where we only belong to each other, not stupid vows to other people.

"We don't have a future; all we have is tonight. I know it's not enough." *It's not enough for either of us.* "But I stand by what I said. I want to fuck you, and then I'll do everything I can to save you."

She nods. "But you'll never belong to me."

It's a statement, not a question, but I nod anyway.

She takes a deep breath. "No."

"No?"

"No, I don't accept your deal. If you want to fuck me, then fuck me. Not because of some deal. I accept that if I let my feelings get involved, it's my own fault. All I'll get is a night of good sex, nothing more. I don't want you to save me in exchange for sex. I don't want anything in exchange for sex."

"What if I ask for naughty, disturbed, embarrassing things?"

She blushes. "That's different. For things I don't want to do, I expect a hero save in return."

I nod darkly. She's wrong if she thinks she doesn't want or enjoy the darker things I want from her. She wants them, but I'd also save her for free. I guess it's fair.

She glances up at the tower where her apartment is. "Want to come up?"

I growl, licking my lips.

She laughs.

I'm out of the car before she can get her hand on her door. She laughs again when I take her hand and start walking into the building. When we get to the elevator, I hit the floor for eleven.

"Do I even want to know how you know where I live?"

"You can ask, but it would probably creep you out, and since you really want to fuck me, I don't think it would be a good idea."

She zips her mouth shut.

The doors finally open on her floor, and I drag her out. She stops suddenly, forcing me to stop so I don't let go of her hand. I've forgotten in the short time I've had without Odette, how it feels to be holding a woman's hand. I like it, maybe too much.

"I don't have my key," Ri says. "Is there a hotel nearby?"

I grin and tug her toward the door. "I don't need a key."

I pick the lock easily, even though it's an intricate lock, and then lead her inside.

The second we are through the door, I finally pounce. If I did earlier, we never would have made it to her apartment. I would've fucked her in the car or an alleyway, and I'm not that much of an asshole. She deserves a proper bed. That and I'm too sore to try to fuck in the backseat of a car like a teenager. I'm too old to screw up my back when there is a perfectly good bed just minutes away.

The second our lips touch, I realize that not fucking her this entire time has been a mistake. She tastes like water after a long drought.

Maybe it's wrong to want someone so soon after loss.

Maybe it's part of the grieving process.

Maybe I'm just a monster.

Or maybe it's because the feelings I had for Odette weren't really love at all, no matter how I felt. Maybe I can't love. I'm not capable of it.

Whatever the reason, I turn off my brain. I won't be needing it anymore tonight. All I need is her.

I tilt her head back as I ram her into the wall, careful not to let her injured shoulder hit. Our bodies line up— my hardness against her soft. Her lips devour mine with delicious strokes of her tongue massaging mine. My hand runs down her body, finding its way under her tank until I find her hips and pull her harder against my body. It's moments like this that I wish I had two hands. Two hands to feel her with, to grab her, to tease her, to make her moan.

My one hand has to work twice as hard, but the way she's moaning, coming completely undone against me, tells me my one hand is more than enough, and we haven't even gotten to the good part yet.

"Freeze, or I'll shoot. And Loki here will rip your balls off," a sassy voice says from behind me.

I stop kissing Ri so reluctantly that I'm afraid I might die if I don't kiss her again in the next five seconds.

"Sorry," Ri whispers with a knowing grin.

"Stop teaching everyone self-defense," I whisper back.

"You brought me here; you could have brought me to a fancy hotel instead," she whispers.

"I wanted you to feel safe," I whisper back.

Her eyes glisten at my words.

I roll my eyes, and then I turn, facing Lucy, Ri's roommate and friend. We haven't met yet, but I knew she'd be here. I just assumed she'd be asleep at three in the morning.

"I'm not hurting her," I say, holding my hand up.

"I don't trust any man with Rialta. Now leave, and I won't call the police," Lucy says, her hand shaking.

I don't leave.

She releases the dog, who does a good job of barking loudly. He'd scare off most burglars, but he doesn't attack. If anything, he retreats a step.

"Loki, attack!" Lucy commands, but the dog just takes a step back and keeps barking.

I use her distraction against her and disarm her in one quick move, taking her gun and pinning her arm behind her back. "I'm Beckett."

Lucy's eyes light up, and I look to Ri.

"It seems that Ri has been talking about me. Good, so you already know who I am and that I'm not her enemy." Lucy struggles in my arm.

"Now, if I let you go, do you promise not to pull a gun on me again?"

She nods.

Slowly, I release her. She looks to Loki. "What good are you?"

The dog comes up to sniff me now that Lucy has calmed down. The large dog licks my hand, and then he finally pounces on me, putting his giant paws up on my chest, which did more than his loud barks ever could.

"Down," I command, and the dog lies down at my feet.

Lucy blinks. "Sure, you behave for him."

Ri laughs. "Sorry, Lucy. Loki is here to make you feel safe, not to actually keep you safe."

"Thanks for letting me know." Lucy huffs. "So he's legit? You two are together?"

"Um..." Ri runs her hand through her ponytail. "We aren't exactly together, but I plan on fucking him if that's what you mean."

Lucy's eyes widen, and she grins. "I'll let you have some privacy then, on the condition that you give me all the details later. And I mean all the details." Her eyes roam my body and then land on my crotch.

I raise an eyebrow at Ri.

"I'll tell you everything later. You're the best." Ri walks over and kisses Lucy on the cheek.

"Just give me a second to change and pack a quick overnight bag," Lucy says.

I pull out my phone to text Hayes while Lucy heads to her bedroom to change out of the men's boxers and Harry Styles T-shirt she was wearing. Hayes and the guys probably followed the tracker in Ri to make sure she's safe. After a couple of quick texts, Lucy is back out into the living room.

"There will be a guy named Hayes in the lobby. Tell him where you want to go, and he'll take you. The hotel is on me, and he'll sleep out in the hallway to ensure you're safe."

"Is he hot?"

I blink, not believing that's all she cares about.

Ri answers, "Yes, Hayes is hot." Ri looks to me. "Lucy doesn't worry about her safety anymore. When we were younger, men would try to kidnap her to get to me, but after Vincent refused to pay the ransom once, they realized that Lucy wasn't a good enough threat. They've left her alone ever since." She turns back to Lucy. "But go with Hayes. He's a good guy. He'll ensure you get settled somewhere."

"He a good fuck?" she asks Ri.

"He knows what to do with his hands," she answers back with a wink.

She's going to pay for that.

Lucy kisses Ri on the cheek and then heads to the door. She opens it, and Hayes is standing in the hallway. She looks back at Ri. "Definitely hot."

Hayes smirks like he knows they are talking about him.

"Oh, and Lucy?" I say.

She stops and looks at me.

"Next time you think a guy is trying to kidnap Ri, just shoot, don't make idle threats."

She smiles. "I knew it was you the whole time. I just wanted to see how far you'd go to fight for our girl. You passed by the way." And then Lucy is tugging on Hayes. "There's a Four Seasons a couple of blocks from here since Mister-can't-keep-it-in-his-pants is paying."

Ri shuts the door, and we can no longer hear Lucy.

"I taught her everything she knows," Ri says.

"Figured."

We stand on opposite sides of the room. As explosive as we were before, we both know that the second we touch each other, any thoughts are going to vanish.

Ri walks to the living room, running her hand over a frame of her giving Lucy Loki as a puppy. The dog in question is still lying on the ground at my feet.

"It's so strange being back here. My memories are still clouded, mixed up from the drugs. Thanks for that, by the way."

I wince, still sorry that the drugs messed her up that badly. They shouldn't have, but then I didn't know her history, or that others would also inject more into her. At the time, I would have done anything to get Odette back.

"It won't help, but I'm sorry."

She ignores my apology, her gaze roaming the apartment. It's not huge, but it's cozy, a perfect place for two single women to live. A small kitchenette that looks like it doesn't do much more than warm up takeout. A two-seater bar and a living room that fits a sofa, small chair, and TV. The bedrooms and bathroom appear to be down the hall.

"This was my safe place for so long. The one freedom Vincent let me have. Live here, work here, go to school here. I always knew it was temporary, but it was still mine, if only for a few years."

A few years. She's only had a few years of freedom. A few years to live on her own. A few years to belong to herself. It was all pretend, all fake. She has always belonged to the mafia, promised to marry another, but this was her sanctuary for a little while.

"The man you were running from, did he come here?"

"No, I've never been kidnapped from here. Vincent

ensured this place is a safe as it can be. Security knows we are here." Her brain is working overtime. "We can't do this," she whispers on a ragged breath.

I cock my head, my heart slamming to a halt at her words.

"Can't? I'm pretty sure Loki won't try to stop us," I try to make a joke to make her smile. I fail.

"I'm forbidden. The guys took a big risk in having sex with me. They did it so I wouldn't be viewed as an object, so I could have some fleeting control. They used masks on the video so it would be harder for Vincent to come after them, but it was still a risk." She looks at me, terrified.

"They were really your first time?"

She nods.

I let that pain roll around in me. I hate that they were her first. Jealous rage courses through my veins.

"Vincent has cameras, security you don't even know about. He'll know we fucked. He'll know you fucked me when I'm forbidden."

"So?"

"He'll remove you from the game."

"He won't, but even if he did, I'm not sure I want to win the game anyway."

She shakes her head. "It's not just the game; he'll kill you for touching me when he forbid it. I can't—"

She's thinking way too much about this.

I move before she has a chance to think more, to worry more.

I take her hand gently, kissing the back of her hand. The single touch has her eyes rolling back in her head.

"I don't care that you're forbidden. I don't care if you belong to me or not. I. Don't. Care. I want you. You want me. Tonight, that's all we are going to worry about."

"But—"

I catch her mouth with mine, shutting her up. She's resistant at first, but I feel her melt into my mouth, her body along with it.

I pull back a second to glance at her. She's still worried, concerned that I'll die. She doesn't know how many near-death experiences I've survived. Death might be a welcomed friend.

"Dying would be worth it for one night with you. If I don't have you, I'll die anyway." I don't know where my words come from, but I know they're true.

There's some strange connection between Ri and me. Something I'm desperate to fully connect. I need her more than anything else. More than revenge. More than a fresh start. More than air.

"I won't come to your funeral," she says with a smirk. Then her arms are wrapped around my neck, and her lips are planted against mine so hard that I stumble a step back.

This time nothing is going to stop us. Death may await me; pain may await her, but neither of us will regret tonight.

18

RI

BECKETT'S WORDS are the most powerful interrogation, capable of making me do anything. They are sweet and beautiful and everything I want to hear, but his words aren't going to be the death of just him; they are going to be the death of me too.

His words add to my ever-growing feelings toward him. I don't understand how these feelings became so consuming so quickly. And yet, my feelings are truer than anything I've ever felt.

My arms are wrapped around his neck, my tongue is deep in his mouth, and I'm lost in him. There is no coming back from this. I'm his.

But he will never be mine, and that is going to fucking hurt. It won't stop me, though. Just like the risk of death won't stop him.

"Why do you have to be such a good kisser, Princess?" he growls as I nibble on his bottom lip.

"Just wait until I fuck you; you'll be saying the same thing about my skills in bed."

He groans as I pull on his lip before bucking my hips

against his hard length straining in his shorts. And then I rub myself up and down his erection. Multiple layers of clothes separate us, but I could come from the friction alone.

His hand is back under my shirt, crawling up my stomach, my ribs, and then under my sports bra until he finds his target—my nipple.

Beckett is an alpha through and through. He likes to be in charge, likes control. I expect him to be rough and demanding, but when he brushes his thumb over my nipple, he's soft and gentle.

There are two very different sides to this man, and I want them both.

The next second he's tugged my bra up, freeing my boobs, and then his head has dipped, taking my other nipple in my mouth so hard that I scream.

He laughs at my reaction. "You're going to wake the neighbors."

I shake my head as my hand fists his hair. "Soundproof walls," is all I can get out. I'm already starting to get incoherent with my words, soon I'll be completely nonverbal.

Then his tongue is ever so gentle against my nipple, licking slowly and soothingly. His hand pinches my other nipple hard, and I gasp.

"I don't know which I like better—your small moans when I'm gentle with you or your loud gasps and cries when I'm rough." He grabs my shirt, removing it gently over my throbbing shoulder, and tossing it to the floor before he does the same to my bra. "I guess I'll have to fuck you twice to find out for sure."

God, yes.

I grab his shirt and rip it over his head before taking

his nipple in my mouth and biting down hard in retaliation.

He moans, and his cock pushes harder against his shorts. I can't resist pushing my hand beneath his waistband and taking him in my palm.

His head rolls back as I palm him—my thumb rubs over the head as I feel the slick precum on his tip.

"Jesus, you have to stop doing that, or I'm going to come before I'm inside you. And I need to be inside you."

I grin triumphantly.

He removes my hand before burying his beneath my leggings, feeling how wet I am. His fingers find their way inside me, pulling my wetness out and rubbing it over my clit.

My knees buckle, and I fall into his chest as I cry out. His fingers don't stop—swirling, flicking, pinching, building me faster and faster.

"Beckett, stop, I'm going to—"

He chuckles. "The magical thing about you, Princess, is that you can come endless times without any problem."

Oh, right.

He presses hard against my clit, and I fall apart. My pants aren't even off, and I'm already coming. The second I'm done convulsing, Beckett has my pants off and is lifting me up. I wrap my legs around him as he carries me toward the bedroom. My lips kiss him furiously as my legs work on kicking his shorts off. We fall naked onto my bed.

"You look better than any princess, Ri. You're a fighter. My fearless fighter."

"Thanks, Hero."

He rolls his eyes.

And then he takes his time kissing every inch of me:

my lips, my neck, my breasts, my stomach—everywhere but where I want him.

"This is torture," I groan. I try to grab his cock, but he's too far away. I try to move his head over my clit, but he dodges my sensitive area.

"Please, Beckett, you're killing me."

"Good, then we can both die together."

My heart swoons at his words. But then concern grows as he kneels over me, his cock finally pressing the sweet spot between my legs.

"Stop. Whatever you're thinking, stop. Just be present with me."

I close my eyes as he kisses me, and worry fills me.

"What is it, Fighter?" he asks, using his new nickname for me.

I don't want to say. It will ruin the moment. We'll stop, and I don't want to stop, not even if what I'm worried about is true.

"Are you worried about protection? Do you have a condom? Are you on birth control?" He strokes my hair and is beyond patient with me even though I can feel how hard he is, how he's trying to ignore the strain in his voice.

"Vincent had me inserted with the implant version of birth control when I was fifteen, and it's been replaced every four years." I hold out my arm so he can see the scar on the inside of my arm where the implant was inserted.

He studies it with a frown, and then he kisses it. Tiny tingles work through my body until I'm curling my toes.

"What's wrong, then?"

"What are you thinking about right now?" I reply.

His frown lines deepen. "That if you don't tell me what's wrong, I'm going to end up doing something very bad like fucking you without your consent. I need you to tell me so I can fix it, and then I can fuck you so hard you'll never worry again. Despite what you think, I'm not that kind of monster."

He plays with my hair while waiting for me to spill my thoughts. His words were a little frantic and needy, but the way he slowly strokes my hair tells me he'd wait for however long it takes for me to tell him.

"Who are you thinking about? Are you...are you thinking about *her?*" I can't say her name. I can't say Odette. But yes, I'm concerned that he's using me, that he's thinking about her. Maybe he needs this so he can pretend I'm her.

"It's fine if you are; I just want to know so I'll be prepared if you accidentally call out her name or something," my words whoosh out of me in one breath.

He grabs my chin, his expression unreadable as he turns my head toward him. "I'm only thinking about you, Fighter, no one else. I already know being with you will be different than anyone I've had before. This is going to feel like a pack of dynamite exploding. It will be that powerful and that wonderful and that painful. With others, it was easy, sweet, and loving. With you, it will wreck us both."

He kisses me hard, bringing me out of my anxious thoughts. His words weren't lies; he gets harder between my legs. His tip pushes just past my entrance, but he's not really inside me, not like I want.

He stops. "You better not be thinking about them when I fuck you," he commands.

"Only you," I croak out.

"Good, now can I fuck you and prove that you're the only woman on my mind?"

I nod.

He pushes past my entrance, and I see stars. Pain slowly turns into pleasure as I take him inside me.

He kisses me, not giving me time to think. Not that I am anyway—my mind is consumed with how big his cock is and how little of him is inside me.

He doesn't tell me to relax, to breathe, or that he'll fit.

Instead, he looks deep into my eyes. He lets me in past his barriers to see what he sees—me. Just me.

His hand runs down my chest slowly and then over the curve of my breast as he freezes inside me. Then his hand dips between my legs until he finds the spot that has me melting at his touch. He doesn't move inside me; he just plays with my clit until I'm on the edge of another orgasm. He stares into my eyes with such warmth that I think he has to be in love with me too.

Dangerous thoughts like that continue to flitter through my head.

He could love me.

I know I love him.

He's the one.

The one that can help me get free.

The one for forever.

But then all the thoughts drift away when he circles my clit, and I scream. I come harder and louder than before, my wetness drenching his cock.

Then he slams inside me, filling me completely.

He rocks in and out of me, his cock sliding all the way in and then almost all the way out. The hard V of his abs now rubs against my clit as his hand plays with my nipple, and his mouth kisses mine.

I feel myself floating out of my body, but I force myself to stay present. I need to remember every second, because this may be the only night I get with him.

With each thrust, it gets harder and harder to not float away, to not explode, but I hold back. I want to wait and come when he does.

I don't see any worry in his eyes about what's in my thoughts.

I guess, technically, I break my promise. For a split second, I do think about the other guys. I think about how even though Beckett only has one arm and one cock, fucking him is ten million times better than fucking all four of the other guys at once. Somehow his one body does things to me that all of them couldn't. He makes me feel like I'm his. He makes me feel wanted, desired, loved in a way I've never felt.

His eyes search mine, and whatever he sees must please him because he thrusts harder, and I can't hold on any longer—my back arches into him.

"Beckett," I cry into his shoulder. My body comes hard on him, rippling pleasure starting in my core and rippling through my fingertips.

"Rialta," he screams back as I feel his warm cum pouring inside me.

There is no denying that the only thing on either of our minds is each other. Fucking changed everything. At least, it did for me.

I shouldn't have fucked him.

I'm not strong enough to let him go. And eventually, I will have to let him go.

He senses the change in me as he pulls out of me. Already my agony is starting to take hold as my body releases him.

He pulls me under the covers and tucks me into his shoulder as I close my eyes to keep from crying, knowing that this isn't real. This was just a really good fuck. One really good night. He doesn't love me. He still loves her, a ghost.

We should fuck again; this is our only chance. But I can't handle him pulling out of me again. I can't handle the loss of him.

He must sense that because he doesn't try to have sex with me again. He just holds me as we both begin to drift asleep.

It's in that weird time between being awake and asleep that the words come to me. I don't know if I actually speak them or just speak them in my mind, but the words exist either way.

"You could win. You could marry me. This could be real."

19

BECKETT

YOU COULD WIN. You could marry me. This could be real.

I know Ri didn't mean to say those words out loud. She was halfway between awake and asleep, and tomorrow she won't remember speaking those words. But still, the words were said.

I heard them.

For a split second, I believed them too.

I wanted her words to be real.

I wanted to win just so I could marry her, not because I suspect her father of killing my wife and need to get back at him through her.

For a second, I let myself imagine that I could have her.

But I've been lost in the fairytale too many times now. My own experiences chasing love have ended in disaster —my friends, who I consider family, have only managed to make it work because they are an anomaly. The odds of a marriage lasting more than a couple of years in this world are slim. Too many become widows. Too many divorce because the job always comes first—it has to if you want to protect your family.

It's why I thought I had gotten out. It's why I married Odette. I thought my life was going to be different.

I squeeze Rialta tighter to my chest and kiss her forehead, breathing in her sweet scent. She's so young, just twenty. She has her whole life before her, and we both know exactly how it will play out.

She will be married off to a man she hates. If she's lucky, the man will treat her with basic respect. If she's not, he'll rape her and beat her. And then, one day, he'll die. Or one day, she'll die. She'll be lucky if she makes it to forty.

It didn't bother me before, her fate. It wasn't my concern. My concern was with getting retribution. But now, my stomach turns just thinking about that life for her.

It doesn't mean she belongs with me. If anything, it confirms the opposite. I will never escape this life no matter how hard I try. I've killed and tortured too many people, made too many enemies.

But her—maybe I could help her find a way to a different life.

I can save her, get retribution for Odette, and try not to destroy her heart in the process. That means I can't touch her again. I can't fuck her. I can't kiss her. I can't play with her. She's already attached; I can't make it worse for her. She has to realize it was just one night, nothing more.

But damn, was it more.

I expected my heart to close off while I fucked her. I expected my heart would break afterward because I would feel like it was far too soon. Odette is barely buried, and I'm already fucking another woman. I thought my guilt would be immense, and it would tear me apart.

Instead, being with Rialta put me back together. Not fully, not enough, but the pieces started aligning. She was the thread carefully stitching me back together. I have no doubt that if I stayed with her, she'd eventually find all the pieces and put me back together until I was whole.

I want Ri, but I don't deserve her. She deserves so much better. I don't know her past; I don't know her history, but I know she's the strongest Corsi—stronger than her father. All she needs is a way out.

I close my eyes, knowing I'm going to need sleep to face tomorrow. But before I drift off, I make another vow. She didn't want to make a deal with me. She wanted sex to be just sex—an ending to a connection we share that neither of us understands.

So I double down on the promise that I made before, the one she didn't accept. This time, I don't want anything in return. I just want to do the right thing by her. Because if I'd met her first, if our paths had crossed earlier—she would have been the one I married. She would have been my everything. I would have stayed in the world for her or given everything up. I would've done anything to make her happy.

Unfortunately, despite all the stitching she did on my heart, I'll always be broken and incapable of love. I'm a monster consumed with taking blood. She's been a nice distraction, but it's time to get back to my goal.

But I can do one last thing for the girl with raven hair who once burst through my life like a freight train set on wrecking everything.

My lips hover over her ear. "I'll save you, forever. I'll play hero as long as you need me. You don't really need me, you're strong as fire, but by the off chance that you do,

I'll do everything in my power to save you—no matter what, Fighter."

———

The sound of my vibrating phone wakes me up. It's a faint sound, but I've always been a light sleeper. I guess having your arm blown off will do that to you.

Ri is still asleep against my chest. I don't want to wake her, but as soon as the phone stops, it starts vibrating again. I need to answer it.

I slip my arm out from under her shoulder and then walk butt naked out of her bedroom. I find my shorts in the hallway that she kicked down my body when she was wrapped around me last night.

I smirk at the memory.

The vibrating phone in the jeans pocket draws my attention. I pick it up.

"Yes?" I half-bark, half-whisper.

"You're an idiot," comes Caius's voice.

"No, I'm your leader, big difference."

He sighs. "You do know going back to her apartment was a big mistake? Corsi has that place monitored more than Riker's Island?"

"I was made aware, yes." I slip my shorts on and walk to her kitchen to see if I can find any coffee or breakfast.

There's one of those Keurig coffee makers. I hate those damn things. They don't make coffee for shit, and these pod fuckers are taking up all the space in landfills.

But I wedge my phone between my head and shoulder and start the machine, guessing that princess and Lucy can't be bothered with learning how to make real coffee. Not that I blame Ri—she's spent all her life being kidnapped, dealing with her fucked up father, and trying to pretend she's a normal kid who gets to go to college and shit.

Lucy, I sort of judge, especially since they work in a cafe.

"Then you know how stupid it was! Corsi is going to kill you for touching his daughter."

"He won't."

"He will."

I shrug. "Then he'll kill me, and you'll take over. I don't see why you have your panties all in a wad."

He sighs. "Can you please try to stay alive longer than five minutes?"

"You hate me; what do you care?" I push the button on the machine and watch as light-colored water comes out. It should be darker, but I don't have time to teach the machine how to make a proper cup of coffee.

"I don't hate you, I just...never mind. I called for a reason."

"Which is?"

"Corsi invited Rialta and me to a dinner tonight to mark the end of our time together."

I go white.

A beep sounds on the machine, and I reach my hand in to grab the coffee. For some reason, the machine thinks I've inserted another cup and starts dripping hot water all over my hand.

"Fuck," I curse as I drop the mug and race over the sink to rinse my hand under cool water.

"Yea, fuck," Caius says.

I turn the water off and shake the water off my hand. I look at the clock that says it's a quarter after eight.

"What time?"

"Seven."

I have less than twelve hours left with her.

It doesn't matter. I can't fuck her again anyway.

I can't do anything with her.

She won't be in my life anymore. She'll be with Corsi, and after the next game, she'll be living with some other guy. My insides boil at that thought. She won't be safe with anyone else. I don't know how Corsi doesn't see that.

"You need to convince Corsi that it isn't safe for her to go with other guys after each game. She needs to stay under his protection."

"I'm sure he'll listen to me," Caius scoffs.

"He listened to us about the game idea."

"That's because he was already thinking about something like it."

I'm not going to be able to keep her safe. I'm going to break my promise in less than twenty-four hours. Now granted, she doesn't know about the promise. She was dead asleep at the time, but still, I know. I want to keep her safe. I'll do anything I can to make that happen.

I'll find a way. I don't break vows. I think about the vows I just made to the Retribution Kings. Okay, I don't break vows that I want to keep, but I want to keep my promise to Rialta.

"What's the plan?" Caius asks, even though I'm sure he and the guys have already thought of one.

"Is everyone at the cabin?"

"Everyone but you, Ri, and Hayes."

"Okay, we'll meet you back there in a little over an hour. Get Gage working on any bugs we can put on you guys that Corsi might not be able to detect, anything we'll need to do surveillance."

"Ri and I can get him talking. We'll find out who killed Odette."

That's what he thinks this is about—finding out who killed Odette. I couldn't give a fuck anymore. All I want to do is keep Ri safe.

I hang up the phone and walk back to the bedroom, where Ri is now lying naked on the bed with her eyes drifting slowly open.

"Morning," she smiles at me like I'm her sun, her moon, her night, like I'm everything she's ever wanted. Like I'm not the man who fucked her with no intention of ever doing it again. Like I'm not the man who's had a vendetta against her and used her position against her. Like I'm not the freaking villain in her story.

I turn my face ice cold. Rip off the bandaid, don't show her any emotion. It's better to hurt her now before she tries to reconnect.

"Get up. We have to leave in five minutes," I bark my orders, then I pull out my phone and start texting Hayes to bring Lucy back so we can all leave.

"Geez, someone is grumpy in the morning." She walks to the bathroom, completely unfazed by my harsh words and leaving me staring at her ass.

God help me, I'm not going to survive her.

———

The ride back to the cabin is uneventful. I stop to get us coffee, since Ri's was disgusting, but otherwise, the three of us don't talk. That might end up being more dangerous because I don't know what snarky thoughts or plans she's making in that pretty little head of hers.

When we get to the cabin, Lennox greets us. "Gage

needs Ri asap. Says he needs to work on devices she can wear without Corsi noticing."

Ri nods and follows Lennox, leaving me and Hayes standing in the living room. He looks at me. "You're a goner. You know that?"

"Huh?"

"You're falling for her."

"I'm not."

He chuckles, adjusting his glasses. "You are. I hung out with you and Odette enough to know what your falling in love face looks like. This is it."

I frown. "I just care about her. I don't want her to get hurt, the same as you, same as any guy in this house. Her life isn't fair. I want better for her. I don't want her. I had my night with her. I got her out of my system."

Hayes shakes his head. "As someone who has had her, you don't just get Ri out of your system. You have her, and she gets under your skin. You don't forget about her."

My hand fists on its own accord as blood pops under my veins, ready for a fight as Hayes continues.

"I'm not in love with her, so relax. I'm not going to fuck her again. I know she's out of my league, and I'm not on her radar. But I know from experience how great she is. She is a catch; she's *the* catch—the one we are all looking for.

"I know you cared about Odette, loved her, and all that shit. But I'm telling you Ri is your match. Ri, not Odette. Ri is strong, fearless, a fighter. She won't put up with your crap or ego. And you need that. Don't let her go."

"Even if all that were true, she deserves better than me."

"She does, and yet, she wants you. She wanted you from the first moment she laid eyes on you."

"The game—"

"Is nothing but an obstacle. Take it from me, don't let her go."

"You're twenty, almost a decade younger than me. What experience do you have in the love department again?"

"Hey, I'm wise beyond my years. I don't have to have experience to see what's in front of my eyes."

Then Hayes leaves me alone. I go plan with Caius, helping him come up with a strategy for their dinner with Corsi. We think of ways to get Corsi talking, ways to keep Rialta safe.

Ri stays with Gage—all damn day. He takes all of her time, or maybe she's purposefully ignoring me. After all, our morning wasn't exactly romantic. There were no kisses, no hugs, no sweet words. It was like two strangers getting ready, not two people who just had life-changing orgasms together.

I finally shower and get ready. Only Caius and Ri were invited, but the rest of us will be nearby in case Ri is in need of rescuing.

I'm combing my hair when there's a knock at my bedroom door. I open it, expecting Hayes to be on my case again. Instead, it's Ri.

I hold the door open for her to come in, despite it being dangerous—her and I in a room alone with a bed again. It's especially dangerous since she's in a silk red dress with fiery red lipstick to match. I have to remind my cock several times that she's not ours; we don't get to fuck her.

She sits on the edge of the bed like she's not phased at all. But then she's eye level with my cock, and that does all sorts of twisted things to me. So I sit next to her.

"It looks like tomorrow will be another game," she says.

"Looks like it," I respond.

She takes a deep breath as if her next words pain her to say them. "I'll find out who killed Odette. Whether it was Vincent or someone else, I'll find out tonight. I'll send Caius back with the information. You deserve to know. And despite Vincent seeming like the worst man on earth, he will tell me."

"How do you know?"

She swallows, and her eyes dart to the door. "I just do."

She's hiding something.

Finally, she looks back at me. "I can get him to talk tonight; then you can get your revenge. Tell Caius to quit the game. He doesn't belong there. He'll just end up dead. And you—you can go back to your life before, to your friends who you consider family."

I don't say anything because she's wrong. I can't go back. There is too much history, too much pain in my past. My friend-family group loves me no matter what. But what I did, what happened, I'll never escape from. This is my life now.

I'll stay in the game as long as possible. Maybe I'll even win.

I tuck a hair behind her ear. She tenses, her eyes closing softly at the simple touch.

"We need to go," Caius says as he walks down the hallway outside our room.

She looks at me like it's the last time she'll ever look at me. "Stay close. When I send the information back with Caius, you'll owe me a save."

20

———

RI

Caius drives slow and cautious, like he doesn't want the car ride to end. I just want him to get to my father's condo and get this over with.

"You're safe," Caius says, reaching over and taking my hand in his. It makes me think of Beckett holding my hand and then having to let go so he could drive. Caius has two hands; he can do both at the same time. It's not fair, but then nothing is fair.

"I won't let Corsi or anyone else hurt you," he continues.

I give him a small smile.

"We won't either," comes Hayes's chipper voice.

I smile a little brighter as I remember that all the rest are listening. Gage is a genius. He figured out how to attach a small microphone in my earring, but it's undetectable to Corsi.

As much as I like Hayes's voice, I much prefer to hear Beckett. I didn't see him most of the day, which was probably for the best. I have to give him up; he needs to escape this world. He's better than it. He's been heartbroken too many times. He lost Odette, lost his arm, and based on the amount of grief that surrounds him, I'm pretty sure he's lost more than I'll ever know.

Not touching him this morning was torture. Not kissing him goodbye was almost impossible.

The guys might think I'm strong because I know how to slice through a man's jugular, but I'm strong because I was able to walk away from Beckett without kissing him. That takes real strength.

We pull up in front of Vincent's building. We both stare up through the windshield at the massive skyscraper.

"Remember when you lost the bet that Beckett got jealous when I kissed you?" Caius asks.

I nod, waiting for Beckett to argue that he wasn't jealous, but he doesn't.

"I'm ready to claim my debt. Kiss me."

He leans over, and I meet his kiss. It's just a kiss. It means nothing. And yet, I wish it could erase Beckett from my body. This kiss is soft, tender, with just the right about of tongue. Some might say it's perfect—but I don't want perfect. I want messy, and rough, and life-altering.

Caius pulls away like I just made him the happiest man on earth with that kiss.

"You ready?" he asks.

I nod.

Adrian comes from inside the lobby to open my door. I climb out, and Caius is immediately at my side, holding his arm out for me. He's dressed in a fitted gray suit. His blonde hair is combed back instead of in the faux mohawk he likes to sport.

Adrian leads us in through the lobby, where Georgio meets us before we get in the special elevator that only leads to Vincent's penthouse.

"Good to have you back, Princess," Georgio says.

"What is Vincent up to?" I ask.

"You know him—just getting to know your suitors better so he can pick the best for you," Adrian answers.

The doors open, and we all step out into Vincent's condo. His butler greets us. "Dinner is already set up in the dining room. If you could follow me, please."

Antonio has known me his entire life, but he still prefers to be formal like I'm a guest here, not a family member.

Vincent is sitting at the head of the table that looks out at the skyline.

"You're late," he says.

"Apologies, Mr. Corsi, I enjoyed my time with your daughter so much that I lost track of time. It's going to be hard giving up such a magnificent creature," Caius says, laying on the charm.

I almost snort but then think better of it. Caius is just playing the part. I should too. Caius winning would be the best outcome. I told Beckett to convince him to bow out gracefully, but I doubt Caius will. He's too kind, too sweet, too protective of me.

"Have a seat," Vincent says, never very good with manners.

Caius leads me to a chair closest to Vincent. He pulls out my seat and helps me sit. Then he takes the seat across from me.

Wine is poured.

Food is served.

Vincent engages Caius in a conversation about how we've been spending our time. Caius doesn't lie per se, but he does bend the truth to make him look favorable. Took me to a cabin getaway. Went boating, taught me how to fish. Showed me what life would be like with the Retribution Kings and introduced me to everyone.

He talks of my beauty and intelligence. About how he enjoyed my company. How our time together was too short all through dinner.

Vincent doesn't show any emotion as we eat, just listening. But I know better. This all feels like a setup; I just don't know what.

"If you will excuse me and Rialta a minute, I want to confirm some details with her myself. Then I'll let you know how you rank in possible suitors for her," Vincent says, getting up from the table. He doesn't order me to follow, but I know that's what he wants.

I give Caius a warning smile. I don't know what's about to happen, but I don't have a good feeling about it.

He frowns but nods his understanding.

When we leave the room, I hear Caius say through the earpiece to the other guys, "Something's up. Be on high alert."

"We're watching you, Ri. We'll move in if Corsi tries anything," Gage says.

I exhale a deep breath. It's not me I'm worried about.

Vincent takes me to his library, which doubles as his cigar room. The books are there mainly as decoration and smoke catchers. It pains me to see so many good books go to waste.

He takes a cigar out and lights it, not bothering to offer me one. For one, women don't smoke cigars. It's not appropriate for a young lady such as myself. And two, he knows I'd use it to burn this entire place down.

"So, what do you think of him?" Vincent asks.

"He's a good guy. Kind, sweet, strong, and he's up for a high leadership position in the Retribution Kings," I try to keep my voice void of emotion. It's too early to show my real feelings or use reverse psychology.

He puffs on his cigar while I sit across from him, picking at my nails and waiting for him to tell me why we really came here. This is also my only chance to get the information I need from him. The guys are going to hate this. I didn't tell them how I'd get the information from him, just that I could.

"I want to make a deal," I say.

Vincent snaps his head to me. "You already owe me one, and you're already willing to owe me twice?"

"Yes."

He blows out smoke. "Let's hear it then, and I'll decide if I want to make a deal."

He can't resist having me owe him one. He's used it against me countless times over the years. I've gained information, but always at a price.

"Tell me who really killed Odette. You say it wasn't you. You say it was Ares, but I don't believe you. I know you know. Who killed her?" I look him dead in the eyes as I say it. It reveals that I have feelings for someone in the Retribution Kings, but we need this information. Beckett needs it. And he needs to get the hell out of here before Vincent kills him.

"I did initially believe it to be Ares. You know I would never lie to you. But I have since learned different. I'll give you the evidence, but you'll owe me the truth—an honest answer to my question. If you lie to me, I'll kill your friend Lucy," he says, waiting for me to accept or deny. He knows I'll tell him the truth. Lucy is too important to me.

"Don't do it," I hear Beckett say. "Don't make any more deals with that monster. We can find another way."

But we can't. This is the only way.

"Deal."

Vincent doesn't react. He doesn't show how pleased he is, but then, he never does.

He walks out, no doubt to his office to retrieve what he needs. This isn't the first time he's made a deal with him where he wanted the truth from me.

"What did you do?" Beckett says, concern dripping.

I saved you. Once you kill the man responsible for killing Odette, you'll be free.

I don't say anything out loud, though.

Vincent returns a moment later with a lie detector device. It's the most sophisticated one available. He doesn't know that I've been practicing for ages to beat it, and I can.

He attaches the sensors to my fingers and then around my chest before he takes a seat opposite me. He holds up a flash drive. "This will show you who killed Odette."

"What's your question?"

"Who did you fuck this week?"

My eyes shoot up. "I didn't fuck anyone." I keep my voice calm, my pulse calm, everything calm.

"Liar," Vincent says without looking at the machine.

"I'm not lying."

"You are."

"Want to do another of your stupid virginity tests to prove it?" I smirk.

"No, we both know those don't actually prove anything. They are just there to deceive the other men." He puffs on his cigar. "But I can sample for any semen inside you and run a DNA test."

He'll do it. If I don't tell him, he'll do it.

I'm screwed.

I need that flash drive.

I need to keep Lucy safe.

But I can't tell him. If I tell him the truth, he'll kill Beckett. If I give any other name, he'll kill them.

"Tell him the truth. Tell him it was me," Beckett says through the speaker in my earring.

I bite my bottom lip. I won't give Vincent Beckett's name. I won't let him hurt him. I have to protect him, just like he's protected me.

"Who was it? I know you fucked someone. You're way too happy to have not."

I raise an eyebrow. "I look happy to you? Really? You put my virginity and marriage up for grabs to the man who can win a game instead of letting me have any say."

"I gave you say with Nicolo and look how that turned out. He's dead."

I have to give him a name. He won't let this drop.

"Who?"

"It was—" I don't know how I'm planning on finishing that sentence, but Caius takes that moment to burst in.

"It was me. I fucked her," Caius says.

"Caius, no," I gasp. Technically, it's true. He did fuck me, just not this week.

"Thank you for your honesty, son." He tosses him the flash drive. Caius catches it and pockets it. But he won't be leaving this room, not unless I save him.

Fuck!

I have to move fast. Vincent won't think long about his punishment. He'll just kill him. He likes the smell of death, likes watching the whites leave men's eyes, likes watching the blood pool and the bodies turn rigid.

I run to Caius, ripping the sensors off as I go. I block Caius with my body just as Vincent pulls out his gun, aiming it at him.

"Don't kill him," I get out.

It's enough to get Vincent to pause.

My emotions are high, and tears are threatening for the selfless thing Caius just did, but I don't know if I can save him.

"I'll do anything; just let him live. Let him finish the game."

"Anything?" Vincent asks.

"Anything. Not just like our other deals. You'll never have to make a deal with me again. Whatever you want, I'll do it. You want me to remove my name, I'll do it. You want me to spy on someone for you, I will. You want me to marry someone, spread my legs, and have his babies, I will. I'll do it willingly. I won't slice my wrists open at the end if this doesn't go my way like we both know I was planning before."

"If you don't, he dies," Vincent says matter of factly, not like he just threatened Caius's life.

"That will ensure I do as you say. Don't kill him." I want to add on Beckett's life and the rest of the guys, but I can't.

"Ri, what are you doing?! Don't do this. We are almost there. We can save Caius, just stall," Beckett says.

But I can't listen to his voice anymore. I have to save Caius. I don't have much to offer Vincent anymore, but I can only trade a life for a life. I can't save Beckett too. Caius saved him. I saved Caius.

I squeeze my earring like Gage taught me in case I thought Vincent was going to find it. My earring flattens, and Beckett's voice disappears.

Caius stiffens behind me, not liking what I'm doing either.

"Deal," I say.

Vincent smiles for once in his life.

He turns his attention to Caius. "It looks like your life has been spared. I'll see you tomorrow night at the game. Good luck to you."

He dismisses Caius, but I'm not sure he'll leave. I turn to face him. "Go, it's okay. He won't hurt me."

"But—"

"Go." I rise up on my tiptoes and kiss the corner of his lips.

He doesn't like it, but when Adrian and Georgio enter, he finally leaves with them.

I look back at Vincent. "You're a fool; you know that? I told you that falling in love would be your death sentence someday."

"I didn't fall in love."

"Sure, you didn't."

He puffs quickly, exacerbated with me. "So you don't want to be forbidden anymore? That was our initial agreement, but it seems things have changed."

I remember our deal. I was the one who wanted to be forbidden from having sex, he didn't care. I thought it would save me. But being forbidden almost killed every man I've ever cared about.

"No, I don't want to be forbidden anymore."

"Fine." He thinks for a moment. "You're no longer forbidden. I'll announce it tomorrow night at the games."

It will save Beckett and the other guys that fucked me. He can't hurt them for touching me, but I know what it also means. I'm no longer off-limits. Whoever wins me can do what they want with me.

"This changes everything," he says, and I don't disagree with him. Beckett won't be able to save me; I'll have to save myself. And sometimes, I'll have to recover after the damage is done. Even I am not strong enough to save myself every time.

Caius is safe.

Beckett is safe.

Gage, Lennox, Hayes—they are all safe.

I smile on the inside. I'll take whatever danger awaits me. They are safe, and Beckett is about to get his vengeance. He's about to heal more than I ever could help him. Then I'll convince him to go, save himself, be free.

One of us should be.

21

BECKETT

WE ARE RUNNING toward the elevators when Caius comes down.

"Where is she? What happened? The feed just cut out," I yell, needing so many answers.

"She turned it off herself."

I frown. "She must be in danger. She must—" I start pushing past him for the stairwell. There is no way the elevators will work for us.

"Stop. She's safe. Vincent won't hurt her," Caius says somberly, like he failed her.

He did.

We all did.

I should thank him. He probably saved my life. But I can't thank him because she gave up her life for him.

I don't know how to save her now. I don't know how to protect her. I don't know how to keep my promise to her.

"We have to go," Lennox says, pulling on me.

"Not without, Ri," I say.

But Lennox and Gage have grabbed me and are dragging me away.

227

"You're in charge, but your feelings are clouding your judgment. Ri is fine. Her father needs her alive. He needs her safe to finish the games. He won't hurt her. You'll see her again tomorrow at the games," Caius says.

I know he's right, but it tears me apart to leave her here with him. *What was I thinking?* I care about her, and I'm not sure I'm strong enough to just give her up.

The guys throw me in the car and drive me to Caius's place in the city. Someone pours me a drink, but I don't take it. I don't want to be numb. I want to feel.

I still can't believe she disconnected us like that. We could be talking to her right now.

I stare at my phone, willing her to text or call. She has my number memorized. She has burner phones. She just has to use them.

Caius approaches after I've appeared to settle down as I sit in the living room, staring out at his shitty view of the city.

"He gave me this." He hands me the flash drive. "I think you should be the first to watch it."

I take the flash drive.

This is what Ri gave up everything for. This stupid thing that's going to tell me who to kill. And once I do get revenge for Odette, it will give me everything—the crown, the power. I'll have the power to choose—stay and be king or leave.

I look to Gage. "There's a laptop in the third bedroom on the right," he says.

I nod and head to Gage's bedroom. I slam the door shut, wanting to be alone for this. This moment I've wanted for so long now feels so unimportant.

I open his laptop and put the flash drive in. I open the single file on it and hit play.

I'm not prepared for what I see.

I should be.

The pieces all fit.

But I'm not prepared.

The video shows Odette in the hotel room.

It shows a person breaking into her hotel room.

It shows a person stabbing her over and over like a skilled assassin.

It shows a person tying her up to wait to be kidnapped by the person's accomplices.

It shows Rialta Corsi is the reason Odette is dead.

Suddenly, retribution is back on the table.

———

Thank you for reading Forbidden Princess! I hope you enjoyed it! Beckett and Ri's story continues in Tempted Hero!

JOIN ELLA'S NEWSLETTER & NEVER MISS A SALE
OR NEW RELEASE → ellamiles.com/freebooks

230

Love swag boxes & signed books?
SHOP MY STORE → store.ellamiles.com

ALSO BY ELLA MILES

LIES SERIES:

Lies We Share: A Prologue

Vicious Lies

Desperate Lies

Fated Lies

Cruel Lies

Dangerous Lies

Endless Lies

SINFUL TRUTHS:

Sinful Truth #1

Twisted Vow #2

Reckless Fall #3

Tangled Promise #4

Fallen Love #5

Broken Anchor #6

TRUTH OR LIES:

Taken by Lies #1

Betrayed by Truths #2

Trapped by Lies #3

Stolen by Truths #4

Possessed by Lies #5

Consumed by Truths #6

DIRTY SERIES:

Dirty Obsession

Dirty Addiction

Dirty Revenge

Dirty: The Complete Series

ALIGNED SERIES:

Aligned: Volume 1 (Free Series Starter)

Aligned: Volume 2

Aligned: Volume 3

Aligned: Volume 4

Aligned: The Complete Series Boxset

UNFORGIVABLE SERIES:

Heart of a Thief

Heart of a Liar

Heart of a Prick

Unforgivable: The Complete Series Boxset

MAYBE, DEFINITELY SERIES:

Maybe Yes

Maybe Never

Maybe Always

Definitely Yes

Definitely No

Definitely Forever

STANDALONES:

Pretend I'm Yours

Pretend We're Over

Finding Perfect

Savage Love

Too Much

Not Sorry

Hate Me or Love Me: An Enemies to Lovers Romance Collection

ABOUT THE AUTHOR

Ella Miles writes steamy romance, including everything from dark suspense romance that will leave you on the edge of your seat to contemporary romance that will leave you laughing out loud or crying. Most importantly, she wants you to feel everything her characters feel as you read.

Ella is currently living her own happily ever after near the Rocky Mountains with her high school sweetheart husband. Her heart is also taken by her goofy five year old black lab who is scared of everything, including her own shadow.

Ella is a USA Today Bestselling Author & Top 50 Bestselling Author.

Stalk Ella at:
www.ellamiles.com
ella@ellamiles.com

www.ingramcontent.com/pod-product-compliance
Lightning Source LLC
Chambersburg PA
CBHW021133190726
48288CB00008B/2642